THE
ARGUMENT

BOOKS BY VICTORIA JENKINS

THE
ARGUMENT

VICTORIA
JENKINS

Bookouture

Published by Bookouture in 2019

An imprint of Storyfire Ltd.
Carmelite House
50 Victoria Embankment
London EC4Y 0DZ

www.bookouture.com

ISBN: 978-1-83888-090-3
eBook ISBN: 978-1-83888-089-7

Dear Diary,

I will die if I don't get out of here. My mother is suffocating me. I feel like every time I try to do anything, she's there, stopping me from living, trying to control me. I don't want to hate her, but sometimes I feel like I do, like hating her comes naturally and is the easiest thing in the world. Sometimes I think she doesn't realise what she's doing, then other times I think everything she does is intentional. Sometimes I think she's enjoying herself, as though making me feel rubbish makes her feel better about her own pathetic life. One of these days I'm going to just walk out of this house. I am going to disappear to a better life, somewhere she won't be able to find me. I'll make myself invisible so that nobody knows where I am, and when I'm gone, it'll all be her fault.

ONE

HANNAH

Rosie is asleep upstairs, tucked up safely in her bed. She is a good girl, she always has been; quiet, content, gentle. Not like her sister. Olivia is everything her younger sibling isn't, wayward and unruly, forever wanting more, always questioning everything. Even in a few years from now, when Rosie will be fifteen – an age Hannah appreciates many parents find challenging – she can't imagine her acting as Olivia does, leaving her here in ignorance, wondering where she is and who she is with, worrying whether she's okay.

For what must be the fifth time now, Hannah tries her daughter's number. This time, it goes straight to answerphone.

'Olivia, it's Mum. It's late now … I'm getting worried. Call me back, please.'

Despite having been told over a week ago that she couldn't go to the party, Olivia has snuck from the house like a thief and gone anyway. She mentioned it while they were all eating dinner together – a passing comment that neither Hannah nor Michael paid much attention to at the time. Hannah didn't think of it again after that, assuming it had been forgotten about. Michael isn't home tonight, and Hannah doesn't drive, and she realises her error in not asking Olivia where this party would be, but she didn't think it necessary when they had made their feelings on the subject so clear. Even if she had access to a car, she has no idea where she might start looking for her daughter. Olivia was told no. Hannah had thought that would be enough.

Is this where it starts? she wonders. She has heard other parents' lamentations; she knows that at a certain age, a certain phase, all teenagers find their feet and start to break away, sometimes gradually, sometimes with one sharp and sudden heave that rips them from their mother and father in a separation that may remain permanent.

It is happening already, Hannah knows that, and yet she has been lying to herself, denying what has been right in front of her all this time. From now on, will she watch her daughter slip away from her, bit by bit no longer her little girl?

She goes into the kitchen and gets herself a glass of water, desperate to rid herself of the headache that pinches at her temples and threatens to swell into a migraine. She wonders if it is normal to feel this old at thirty-four, or if it is simply the effect of having had children young. She knows she looks older than she is; she always has done. When she met Michael, she was seventeen, but he thought she was in her twenties. It was something she was always quietly smug about back then, this looking older than she was, but now that time is really upon her and has started to move quicker in recent years, she wishes the reverse were true. How nice it would be to stop time, she thinks; not just for herself, but for her daughters too. Given the chance, she would have paused it a few years back, before Olivia became the way she is now.

The clock fixed to the wall above the microwave tells her it is already gone 10.45. Refilling her glass with water, she takes it into the living room and returns her attention to the iPad she has borrowed from Michael's office along the hallway. She knows the names of some of the girls in Olivia's school year, though she has never known her daughter to bother much with any of them. Olivia is a loner; she always has been. Hannah has no idea whose party it is; Olivia may have mentioned the details when she brought the subject up last week, but Hannah doesn't remember what was said. Despite everything, she believed her little girl was still in there somewhere, caught amid the attitude and the defiance, and she naïvely thought she would never defy her wishes in this way.

She types the name of one of Olivia's classmates into Google and waits for the results to load. She finds the girl on the second page, an Instagram account that is open for browsing to anyone who might chance upon it. Hannah isn't particularly good with social media; it has never been something that interests her. Facebook was still in its infancy when Olivia was born, and although by the time Hannah gave birth to Rosie everyone seemed to be using it, she was up to her eyes in newborn paraphernalia and the debris that came with an active five-year-old, and the last thing she had time for was taking a peep at other people's lives.

Her eyes widen at the sight that is Casey Cartwright's Instagram profile picture. Hannah doesn't understand what Instagram is, how it works or what the point of it is, but from what she sees here, it appears to offer a platform for its users to flaunt anything that involves excess. It amazes her that the girl's parents let her parade herself on the internet as she does. This photograph, available for anyone to see, shows Casey posing on a dance floor, her rear end jutting to the camera in a dress so tight it appears to have been painted on. Her head is turned to the person taking the photograph, her mouth parted in a consciously provocative and simultaneously gormless gape. She is just fifteen or sixteen years old, and everyone knows that these social media sites are dangerous places. It is easy for a person to pretend to be someone they're not. The girl is leaving herself open to all kinds of trouble, and no one seems to be there for her to stop it from happening.

Though she knows her own daughter isn't on Instagram, Hannah types in Olivia's name, just to be sure. It wouldn't surprise her to find that she has opened an account somehow, if only to get at her parents in some way, but she is grateful when she doesn't find her daughter among the list of other females of the same name. Olivia is showing an ounce of common sense where this is concerned, at least.

At her side, her mobile phone bleeps. It is a message from Michael.

Sorry I haven't called. Long day. Off to bed now – early start. Everything okay back home? X

Michael rarely calls when he's away with work; Hannah doesn't expect him to be constantly in touch, not when his workload is so demanding and the trips so stressful for him. Two years ago, he was promoted to senior director with the supermarket chain he has worked for since she met him, and the role has involved extensive travel within the UK. The meetings he attends sound long and tedious, and in the moments when he is in between work, she doesn't blame him for taking some time out for himself. She knows she would do the same if she was ever given the chance.

She looks at the message. She knows she should tell Michael what has happened – that Olivia has gone to that party – but it would only worry him. He is in Southampton, hours away from their home in Penarth, in South Wales, too far to be able to do anything useful to help the situation, so what would be the point in spoiling his evening by causing him unnecessary concern? Instead, she sends him a reply that suggests everything is as normal.

All fine here. Hope you get a good night's sleep. See you tomorrow. X

When the message is sent, she tries Olivia's mobile phone again.

'Olivia, this isn't funny. You've made your point. You need to come home now.'

She turns on the television and stares blankly at the muted screen for a while but is unable to keep herself distracted from the collision of thoughts that has exploded in her brain. What if something happens and she can't get hold of Olivia? What if her daughter is alone and hurt somewhere, and no one knows that something has happened to her?

Stop it, Hannah. She is allowing herself to overthink, letting her brain imagine the worst when she knows that the most likely end to her worry will be the sight of Olivia nonchalantly approaching the house as though this is just any other evening. She will know that she has done wrong, but she'll do everything she can to present a couldn't-care-less attitude designed to irritate Hannah further.

It is while she is considering this scenario that exactly this happens. At 11.20, the outside sensor lamp at the front door clicks on, illuminating the driveway in a puddle of soft white light. Olivia emerges from the stone pathway like a ghost, her footsteps crunching across the chippings. Her hair is pulled back messily, piled up on her head, and her face looks paler than usual. Hannah can't deny how slight how daughter looks, caught like this in the muted lighting. In recent months she has begun to fade away, refusing food and becoming a shadow of her former self. Hannah worries, though she suspects that it is yet another way in which Olivia is seeking rebellion.

She waits to hear the tap-tap-tap of her daughter's knuckles on the front door before letting her into the house. Olivia steps past her wordlessly, stumbling to one side, and stoops to take off her shoes. She finds it hard to balance, and when her shoes are off and she is upright again, she refuses to make eye contact.

'Where have you been?' Hannah doesn't know why she asks this when she already knows the answer. She realises now that the previous week's 'Can I go to the party?' meant 'I am going to the party.'

Rather than reply with the obvious, Olivia offers her a shrug, and even that is given grudgingly. She is wearing make-up that has smudged beneath her eyes, casting dark shadows, and it makes her look older than she is, world-weary in a way that suggests it is possible to be defeated at just fifteen.

'I came back, didn't I?'

Her words are slurred, and when she moves to head towards the stairs, Hannah stops her, reaching for her arm. 'In there,' she says, gesturing to the living room.

Olivia sighs loudly, the exhalation enough for her mother to catch the sickly scent of alcohol that lingers on her breath. Has she really been drinking? It seems obvious that she might have been when no doubt everyone else at the party is likely to have done the same. Hannah feels her frustration grow.

She closes the living room door behind them, not wanting to disturb Rosie. 'What's going on?'

Olivia folds her arms across her chest and turns her head to the darkened television, as though staring at a blank screen is preferable to engaging in an exchange with her mother. The framed photograph on the mantelpiece catches Hannah's eye. It is a picture of the girls, Olivia aged eight and Rosie then just three years old. Olivia is wearing school uniform: green cardigan top-buttoned over a grey pinafore dress; beside her, Rosie wears a grey dress of her own, though she has not yet graduated from nursery and is too young to be wearing the same uniform as her sister. Even before she could speak, Rosie expressed a desire to be just like Olivia, following her around the house and mimicking her gestures. She would pull at her red curls, trying to straighten them out so that her hair would look just like Olivia's. By the age of five, though, everything had changed, and Rosie had abandoned her adoration of her sister. Perhaps even then she was able to see what was becoming of Olivia.

'You went to that party,' Hannah says, a statement rather than a question.

Olivia shrugs again, answering her with silence.

'We told you not to go.'

'It was no big deal,' she says, looking at the floor. 'It was a house party, that's all.'

'I don't care what or where it was. The fact is, we told you that you couldn't go, and you went anyway.'

'Why does it matter so much?' The words are spat in temper, and Olivia studies her mother with contempt, holding her eye with an unspoken challenge.

'If you have to ask,' Hannah tells her calmly, 'then you already know.'

Olivia rolls her eyes. Hannah hates it when she does that. It represents everything she never wanted her daughter to become, petulant and disrespectful, and though she feels sure that many well-intentioned people might try to reassure her that Olivia's attitude comes with being a teenager, she doesn't know how long it is going to be reasonable to use her age as an excuse for her behaviour.

'Why was it so important to you to go?' Hannah asks.

'Everyone else was going.'

It is Hannah's turn to roll her eyes as she despairs at her daughter's childish argument. Olivia notices the look and huffs loudly, clamping her teeth on to her bottom lip as though forcing back something she wants to say.

'And if everyone else does drugs,' Hannah says, 'is that also something you want to try? Or what about getting pregnant? Sound appealing if everyone else is doing it?'

The exasperation that floods her daughter's features is tangible. Hannah knows what it is that Olivia would like to say, but she knows that even despite her recent attitude, she wouldn't be cheeky enough to come out with it. She knows what Olivia thinks of her, that she is over-the-top, controlling, but having tried every other way to make her see sense and failed to get her to so much as acknowledge her attempts, she has little choice other than to deal with her daughter in her own obtuse manner.

'Maybe it does,' Olivia says, widening her eyes. She is goading her mother, pressing her until she gets a reaction.

'Did you enjoy it?' Hannah asks. Olivia eyes her suspiciously, wondering where the question is headed. Her focus flits from one side of Hannah's face to the other as she tries to formulate an answer, as though trying to settle on the least incriminating response. It really isn't a trick question; Hannah is curious to know whether the party lived up to her expectations.

'It could have gone better.'

'In what way?'

Olivia pauses. Her mother can read her as though the things she doesn't want to say are tattooed across her forehead, printed in bold lettering for everyone to see regardless. Something has happened; she has done something, something she doesn't want Hannah to find out about.

'I'm just different, aren't I?' Olivia says, and Hannah suspects the comment is an evasion of a truth she doesn't want to admit to. 'People laugh at me. They laugh at how I dress.'

'What's wrong with how you dress?' Hannah looks Olivia up and down, taking in the jeans and T-shirt, wondering what anyone might find amusing in the very normal clothes her daughter is wearing. The jeans are too big for her, hanging slightly around her hips, but not in any way that might be regarded as unintentional.

Her attention isn't away from Olivia's face for long enough to miss the eye-roll she is offered in response to the question.

'You just don't get it, do you?' Olivia snaps, studying her mother as though a second head has sprouted from her shoulders and she is unsure to which of them she should direct her anger. 'God,' she continues, 'you're not even that old.'

'Meaning?'

'Urgh,' she says, throwing her arms in the air, exasperated by her mother's refusal to rise to her bad mood, because that is what she is looking for. She seems to enjoy confrontation, actively looking for opportunities to get into an argument with Hannah over something, no matter how trivial the subject. She is the same with her sister at times, moody and cantankerous, trying to wind Rosie up at any available opportunity.

'Other parents get it. Other girls my age get to wear nice stuff; they get to go to parties.'

Hannah thinks of Casey Cartwright's profile picture, the image like a still from an X-rated adult film. Is that what her daughter aspires to? Is that what all her parenting has been for, so Olivia can join the herd and follow everybody else in their mundanity?

'Nice stuff,' she repeats. 'Like Casey Cartwright, you mean? Was she at the party tonight?'

Olivia narrows her eyes questioningly, an expression she seems to wear much of the time. 'What are you bringing her up for? What do you know about Casey Cartwright?'

'I've seen how she dresses, that's all. Her Instagram profile picture should come with a parental guidance warning.'

Olivia glances at the iPad on the arm of the sofa, her face contorting as though she's just received life-changing news.

'You've been looking at her Instagram?' Her voice rises and her cheeks flush pink. 'Oh my God, you are so embarrassing.'

'What's embarrassing about that? She's not going to know.'

Hannah knows why Olivia is angry with her. She isn't interested in fashion; she doesn't wear much make-up; she can't remember the last time she bought a new pair of shoes. If she were to dress up, though, Olivia would probably be mortified. No matter what she does, she won't win.

'Would you have gone tonight if your father was home?'

Olivia says nothing.

'I'm going to tell him, you know that, don't you?'

Olivia's dark eyes narrow again, and her top lip thins. She eyes her mother defiantly. 'Tell him what you like,' she says, her words laced with a challenge. 'I don't care.'

Hannah raises an eyebrow and puts out a hand. 'Your phone.'

Olivia scrunches her face as though she has just bitten into something sour. 'You can't.'

Hannah raises the eyebrow further; the look alone is enough. Olivia reaches into her pocket to retrieve her mobile phone, before slamming it into her mother's open palm.

'I hate you,' she hisses. 'You've ruined my life.' She marches to the living room door and yanks it open before turning back, her mouth moving to say something she doesn't seem capable of articulating, a million and one words that are sitting on her tongue ready to be fired at her mother. Instead, in a voice that is disconcertingly calm, all she says is, 'I'm never speaking to you again.'

She slams the living room door shut behind her before heading upstairs. Hannah hears her heavy steps tramp across the landing and her bedroom door thud shut. There is no thought for Rosie, who is sleeping in the room next door. There is no thought for anyone but herself. If Hannah could put her behaviour down to just being a teenager, she would, but where Olivia is concerned, she fears there is something more, something they are only now beginning to see the start of.

TWO

OLIVIA

Her head hurts. She drank nearly three glasses of wine at the party last night, even though she hated the taste of it. She had tasted wine before – she stole some of her parents' months earlier, sneaking downstairs during the night and trying it through a frustrating combination of curiosity and boredom – but just a couple of sips had been enough to deter her from bothering again. Last night felt different, though. Last night, for the first time ever, she felt as though she might be able to fit in somewhere, if only she was given a chance. People laughed at her, but Olivia is so used to that now that she was almost able to block out the sniggers and the comments whispered behind raised hands, ignoring them with a determination that does not usually come naturally to her. She knows she will have to change to fit in anywhere, but the idea of changing only seems to be a good thing.

She stares through glassy eyes at the Artexed ceiling, the swirling white patterns making her headache worse. She has done this so often over the years, during all her time spent in this bedroom, seeing shapes and figures in the twists and turns that play out above her: a dragon with its long tail looped around itself; a bird taking flight from the branch of a tree; a face with blurred features that watches over her as she tries to find sleep amid her thoughts. She pushes the duvet down to her waist and lifts her pyjama top from her chest, allowing the air to circulate and cool her sticky skin. She would love to open a window, to feel a burst of fresh air against her face. For now, she stays where she is, replaying in her head what happened at the party last night and the argument she had with her mother when she got home.

She lies beneath her duvet for what feels like forever, her thumping head made worse by the anger that throbs through her like a second beating pulse. She feels so much of it that she thinks she might explode, and she wonders how her mother would feel then, to come upstairs later to find nothing left of her, just a mess of pieces blown apart by the suffocating dictatorship her parents insist on inflicting upon her. It would serve her right.

She stares at the wallpaper and the embossed patterns that can still be made out through the paintwork. A few years back, she had begged her mother to have her room redecorated. Childish fairies and toadstools had still adorned the walls, having been there since she was just a little girl. No matter how much her mother might have wanted to keep her young, Olivia was growing up. In places, where the paint was applied too thinly and could have done with another coat, traces of the animations can still be seen, like some relic of the past, her mother still clinging to a childhood that has gone.

Olivia doesn't want to be reminded of her childhood. When she sees these patterns through the paint, it is like looking at ghosts from the past, things she doesn't want to have to be subjected to. She isn't a little girl any more. Just months from now, she will be old enough to do so many things she knows her mother is desperate to keep her from, but there will be nothing she can do to stop her, not now that Olivia has decided things need to change around here.

There is a knock at her bedroom door, and the irony of the gesture makes Olivia's hands curl into small fists at her sides. On any normal day there wouldn't be a thought for her privacy, but she realises that this is not like any normal day. Her mother wants her to call out to answer her; this sudden knocking on the door to announce her presence on the other side is nothing more than a trick to get Olivia to speak. She won't do it. She made a threat, and she intends to carry it out. Ignoring the sound, she turns onto her side and faces the wall.

'I'm coming in,' her mother says, when the third knock at the door goes unanswered.

Olivia closes her eyes at the sound of her mother entering the room, bracing herself for the lecture she knows is to come. There have been so many of these talks that they have all started to merge into one. The general message is always the same: don't do anything remotely exciting; don't break any rules or dare to do anything that might involve having what is commonly known as fun. Olivia wonders not for the first time whether it is possible to die of boredom. If it hasn't been achieved by anyone yet, she believes she may be monotony's very first victim.

'You don't want to stay in bed all day, do you?'

Her mother stands behind her, trying to taunt her with the question and with the answer she knows Olivia will not give, and Olivia can sense her presence looming there like some harbinger of doom. They talked about them in an English lesson once at school, these people or things that arrive like a bad omen, and it occurred to her at the time that the description fitted her mother in so many ways.

'I think you should come down and have some breakfast, at least. You haven't eaten anything since yesterday.'

When she feels her mother's hand on her shoulder, Olivia has an urge to hit it away. She won't give her the satisfaction of seeing a reaction. This is what her mother wants, to goad and test her, to see how far Olivia can be pushed before she will break. Her mother would love to see her lash out, because then she could argue that her point has been proven: her daughter is nothing but trouble, out of control. She herself would become the poor victim, the woman whose wayward daughter assaulted her, with Olivia forever condemned as the evil horror-film-cliché offspring.

'I only want what's best for you.'

Her mother's fingers press against her shoulder, massaging her skin. Olivia grimaces. She holds her breath, not wanting to slip up and say what is stuck at the end of her tongue; not wanting to end so soon what she has only just started. Now that she has made the promise – to her mother and to herself – she needs to see it through.

'I know you don't feel it,' her mother continues, refusing to give up, 'but you're still young. You think I don't get it, but I do. And when you're older, when you've got kids of your own maybe, you might finally understand me too.'

When her mother's hand leaves her, Olivia draws in breath through clenched teeth. She just wants to be left alone; is that so much to ask? She will never have children; she isn't sure why anyone would want to. Why would she want to be a parent, when all parents seem to do is mess things up?

'There's food downstairs for you when you're ready.'

She waits for her mother to go, relieved at the sound of the bedroom door being pulled closed behind her. Then she turns onto her back again, refocusing on the patterns on the ceiling. She thinks about what happened the night before and feels a flush that rises to her cheeks. She thinks about that boy, about what they did – what she did – and she imagines telling her mother, watching the reaction on her face when she hears about what really went on at that party. It would be worth whatever trouble she got into just to see the look on her face.

Olivia needs to get out of here. She needs a plan. Her head hurts more as she thinks too deeply, and she knows that she can't do this now; she needs more sleep first. She needs to sleep through the ache that tugs at her head and the numbness that pulls at her legs until she finds herself able to get up again and face the world. Lost to a daydream of a different life, somewhere far from this place they call home, she finds her eyes growing heavy and she loses herself to the fantasy of being somewhere else. Of being someone else.

When she sleeps, the dream doesn't go with her. It never does.

A couple of hours later, she is roused by the sound of more knocking at the bedroom door. Her head remains fogged with the effects of alcohol, and her limbs feel heavy, her ankles still weighted to the bed. There is a second bout of knocking. Her mother is persistent if nothing else, she thinks.

'Olivia.'

It is her father, home from his work trip. He has been away for three nights, though it feels like longer this time around.

He knocks again, a slow, repetitive beat played out on the bedroom door.

'I'm going to come in, okay?'

She doesn't answer him; it isn't really a question.

'Is everything all right?'

If he knows she went to the party last night, he isn't giving anything away, not yet. His calmness makes Olivia suspect that her mother hasn't told him that she snuck out of the house, though she's not sure why she wouldn't. Her mother loves playing telltale to Olivia's father, letting him know just how awful she is. Yet in this case, perhaps she doesn't want to admit what happened. Telling him will mean confessing to her own ineptitude, and why would her mother want to do that?

The bed sinks to one side as her father sits on the edge of the mattress. Turned to the wall, her back to him, Olivia cringes.

'Come on, Liv, what's this all about?'

She hates it when he calls her that. Her parents think she's stupid, but she's not ignorant enough to miss the irony of the shortened version of the name they chose for her. Liv. Live. Exactly what she's not doing, not while they keep treating her like a little kid and trying to rule her life.

'Your mother's upset that you won't speak to her.'

Olivia doubts that very much. Her mother doesn't get upset; she's far too emotionless for that. She wonders what her mother has told her father, what explanation she has provided for why Olivia is refusing to talk to her.

'It's a beautiful day out there,' he says, though Olivia is sure that this is also a lie. When she came home the night before, the sky was black with the heavy threat of rain. She could smell it in the air, dank and strangely cleansing.

'You should get out in the garden.'

She rolls her eyes with the irony of his suggestion. The garden isn't far enough; if she goes outside, she wants it to be somewhere a long way away from here.

'I brought some cake home with me,' her father continues. 'I picked it up from the bakery in town, that lemon drizzle they do. I know you love that one. Come on, Liv, what do you say? Slice of cake and a cup of tea?'

She used to like that cake once, when she was about twelve, when she had hips that were wide enough to balance plates on. She hasn't eaten cake in over a year, but her father obviously hasn't noticed that. It seems he only pays attention when he wants to stop her from doing something. One look at a slice of sponge and she seems to pile on five pounds. It was her parents' fault she was an overweight child, too chubby to ever be involved with the pretty girls' conversations and too slow to be chosen for a team during PE lessons; they were forever trying to tempt her with treats and snacks, always bribing her with food to get her to behave in the way they wanted. They wanted her to be fat and ugly, just like they never want her to have any fun.

'Your mother loves you,' he continues, 'and so do I. We've only ever tried to do our best for you.'

Olivia rolls her eyes. She waits for what comes next – the 'after everything I've done for you' speech, or the 'there are children in the world who'd give their right arm to have your life' one. The comment she waits for never comes. Instead, her father goes to the bedroom doorway, where he turns to her. 'Call if you need anything. You'll have to speak to us at some point, Liv.'

But he is wrong. He is so wrong. She never has to speak to either of them again.

THREE

HANNAH

The afternoon passes quickly, household chores keeping her occupied enough to stop her mind from lingering too long on Olivia's persistent silence. Olivia stays in her bedroom for the whole day, refusing to speak to anyone and declining all offers of food. It is a dry day, a little chilly, but the sun is struggling to make itself visible in infrequent bursts, so Rosie has taken herself to the end of the garden, the hood of her cardigan pulled up over her head, red curls escaping, and her mind lost in the pages of the book she is reading.

Michael comes into the kitchen and flicks the switch on the kettle.

'She's still not speaking to me,' Hannah tells him.

He shrugs, and she feels her jaw tighten at the gesture. 'Don't you find it odd?'

'Not really, love. She's a teenager.'

'We can't put everything down to her age.'

He steps towards her and slips an arm around her waist, rubbing a palm on the small of her back. 'Stop worrying,' he says, in that same voice that is usually a source of reassurance. 'She'll soon come around.'

He kisses her forehead and returns to his task of making tea. Hannah isn't so sure he's right this time. Something feels different, as though some conflict has been declared. Olivia is using this silence as a weapon with which she intends to wreak destruction.

Hannah pours a glass of orange juice and takes it out into the garden, but stops at the start of the lawn before Rosie notices her there. Legs crossed and hood up, her younger daughter is like a little pixie at the bottom of the garden; she is a picture taken from a book of fairy tales, magic spun in the air around her. Hannah smiles. If she could freeze time, keep Rosie in any way, it would be this.

She turns and glances back to the house, looking up to the closed curtains of Olivia's bedroom. She wishes her older daughter could be more like the younger, though she knows that two siblings are rarely alike. What trouble will Olivia bring them in the future? Hannah has worked so hard for this family, doing her utmost to make a safe and secure home for them all. How is she to be thanked for everything she has done?

She walks down to the bottom of the garden and holds out the glass to Rosie.

'Thank you.'

'Can I get you anything else?'

'No thanks.'

Hannah rubs a hand on Rosie's arm before standing and returning to the house. Glancing up at the window of Olivia's bedroom again, at the curtains that remain pulled shut, blocking out the daylight, she wonders how long she will stay there.

When she returns to the house, Michael is back in his office finishing his end-of-week paperwork. He likes to be alone in silence when he works; it allows him to get things done quicker so he can return to spending time with the family. Hannah realises she should probably enjoy these quiet, peaceful moments when her chores are completed and the girls are at home, but she isn't sure that she does. When she is home alone during the week, she often plays music, losing herself to old nineties classics while she gets on with whatever needs doing that day. The house is quieter at weekends, as Michael prefers it that way, but where there is silence there is time to think, and thinking is something that has never ended well for Hannah.

She finishes the ironing, and by 9 p.m. Rosie has gone to bed. Michael still hasn't emerged from his office. She makes him another cup of tea and something to eat, and takes it down the hallway, knocking on the door and waiting for him to respond before entering.

'You okay?'

'Mmm.'

She waits for him to ask her the same back, but he doesn't. She wants to be asked; she needs an opportunity to tell him that no, everything is not okay, but she knows he doesn't want to hear it. She wants him to hold her. She needs reassurance, and the place she has always found it is Michael.

'I made you a sandwich.'

'Thanks, love. Just leave it there,' he says, not turning to her. 'I won't be much longer; just wanted to get this lot finished so I don't have to do it tomorrow.'

She watches him for a moment, his back to her, wondering when he started to look different, and how she hasn't noticed until now. His thinning hair is sparse at the top of his crown, and he has filled out around the waist, the onset of middle age catching up with him early.

'Okay. I'm going to go to bed, though,' she tells him. 'I could do with an early night.'

'Okay,' he replies, his attention still on the screen of his laptop.

She waits a moment longer, and sensing her hovering at the door, he swivels around in his chair. She sees the man she fell in love with still there in his face, in the light of his eyes and the tilt of his mouth, and she feels a surge of gratitude for this life that they have built together, which cocoons her in all its comforts. She feels guilt for her recent doubts, doubts that have plagued her sleep and continued to haunt her during her waking hours.

'See you in a bit.' He gives her a smile she's unable to read before returning his attention to his laptop.

As Hannah eases the door shut, she hears him call her back.

'Go to Olivia's room,' he tells her.

'I thought we were leaving her for a while?'

He shakes his head and turns away from her, the conversation over.

Hannah goes upstairs and does as he has requested. Olivia pretends to be asleep, her body turned to the wall, though Hannah knows when she is faking it; she can tell from the way she is lying. Olivia sleeps on her back; she has done since she was a baby.

She goes into the room briefly, her movements swift as she adjusts Olivia's duvet over her feet. She waits for some sort of response or reaction, but Olivia lies inert, continuing in her defiant silent protest, not so much as pulling her legs up to move them away from her.

'Night, Olivia,' Hannah says softly, but there is nothing offered in return.

The door to Rosie's room is ajar, and she pushes it open gently, poking her head into the room to listen to the sound of her younger daughter's breathing. Then she goes to the bathroom to brush her teeth and take off her make-up – just a thinly applied layer of foundation and a flick of mascara on each eye. She tries not to linger on her face for too long in the mirror, on the new lines that crawl from the corner of each eye and the dark circles that rest beneath them, concealed until now by the creamy foundation she wears like a shield to protect herself. She has an outbreak of spots on her right cheek, a condition that always afflicts her whenever she suffers any stress.

In the half-light of the bedroom, she changes into a nightdress, then slips beneath the duvet. She closes her eyes but finds herself unable to sleep. When Michael comes upstairs, she listens as he undresses in the dark, wondering whether she might pretend to be asleep. She has always been useless at it.

The bed shifts as he climbs under the duvet beside her.

'Thought I could do with an early night as well.'

He presses his body against hers, the heat of his skin warming her, and now she knows what that smile in the office was all about. When his hands pass over her thighs and push her nightdress up, she feels herself flinch at his touch. She is being unfair, she knows she is; it's not him, it's her. Sex hasn't been appealing in a long time; in fact, she can't remember the last time they were intimate. She can't even explain to herself what causes it, but there is something in Hannah that throws up a barrier every time the opportunity for physical closeness arises. He has been patient with her, understanding, but she is sure there is only so long he will wait for her. And yet he has waited for her before.

His hands run over her waist and reach her breasts. He kisses the nape of her neck and she responds by tilting her head back, trying to block the negative thoughts that have crept into her brain like a mass of tiny spiders. She tries not to focus on her weight as he touches her: the extra flesh around her thighs; the loose skin that sags at her stomach. She loves being a housewife, a stay-at-home mum, but she knows that she has let herself go and is old before her time. Being a grown-up once felt safer, so much steadier than the uncertainty of her youth, but in recent years she has felt differently about it.

The sex is functional; she imagines that he enjoys it more than she does. When he is done, Michael turns on his back and places a hand on her shoulder; she waits for him to say something, and when he doesn't speak, it comes as a relief to her.

She drifts in and out of sleep, her mind restless and her dreams vivid. She wakes at around 2 a.m., this time unable to fall back into her slumber. She thinks she might have heard something, but she can't be sure whether it was in her own head; the noise of a dream, too real and too loud. And then she hears something else, a sound like a smash, distorted by the lethargy of her sleepless state. She is a light sleeper, she always has been, and when her thoughts aren't already responsible for keeping her awake, it takes little to pull her from her dreams. She pushes herself up on an arm, her eyes adjusting to the darkness of the room. The bedroom door is open slightly – she got up earlier to go to the bathroom and didn't click it closed for fear of disturbing Michael – but there are no lights on; just a sliver of a glow from a street lamp that pushes through the crack in the curtains to help her make out the familiar shapes of the furniture.

There is another noise, a bang. Hannah sits up now, her heart pounding painfully beneath the thin cotton of her nightdress. Sometimes the fridge makes noises that are loud enough to wake her; it has been doing it for a while now, this random clanging and clunking, and she is certain it won't be long before it needs replacing. Yet this sounded different, not like any noise she has heard in the dead of night before. There is someone downstairs, someone in their home.

'Michael,' she says, putting a hand on his bare shoulder and shaking him. 'Michael.'

She waits a moment, listening to make sure she hasn't imagined it, but she knows she didn't. There is silence, but she senses that whoever is down there is trying to be quieter now, having realised their mistake in making so much noise. Hannah feels her heart continue to thud, a blend of adrenaline and fear sending her pulse into overdrive.

'Michael,' she says again, gripping him more tightly and hissing in his ear. 'There's someone downstairs.'

He grunts and puts out an arm, groping in the darkness for her. 'What's the matter?' he asks through sleep.

'There's someone downstairs,' she repeats.

This time he sits up and turns to her, putting a reassuring hand on her arm to try to calm her down. 'Were you dreaming?'

A clattering from downstairs answers his question without Hannah having to speak. He clambers from the bed and pulls on the trousers he left on the chair in the corner just hours earlier. 'Wait here,' he tells her as he goes to the door, but she is already out of bed and following him out onto the landing, ignoring his request to stay put.

Michael moves slowly, edging tentatively towards the top of the stairs. It has fallen quiet again downstairs, as though there was never anyone there at all, and Hannah wonders for a moment if whoever was there has heard them and is already gone. She wonders if she really did hear anything, or if her mind was playing cruel tricks on her, the memories that have plagued her thoughts now infiltrating the present.

'Olivia,' she hears her husband say.

She looks past Michael and sees Olivia standing on the stairs in her pyjamas, her hand clutching the banister.

'Get back up here,' Michael tells her.

For once, Olivia does what her father asks her without argument. She steps onto the landing and passes Hannah wordlessly, avoiding eye contact. She looks so pale in the half-light, wan and ghostlike, a shadow of the girl she was just this time last year. She goes soundlessly into her room and closes the door behind her.

Hannah follows Michael down the stairs; she has more important things to focus on than her daughter's silent protest. She watches as Michael picks up an ornament from the hallway table: a tall ceramic vase she has never really liked and can't remember how she came by. He passes the living room; the door is open, and though the room is bathed in darkness, it is possible to see that everything is as it was left the night before.

The kitchen is at the back of the house, knocked through into what was once a separate dining room. This part of the house is Hannah's pride and joy, the renovation gifted to her by Michael as a ten-year-anniversary present.

Michael raises the vase above his shoulder as his free hand moves to the kitchen door handle. He pushes the door open with a firm shove, stepping back and gripping the vase in both hands now, ready to swing it if necessary. They wait, but there is no sound; no intruder comes charging towards them as Hannah feared they might. The room is thick with darkness, and Michael steps forward again to flick the light switch.

There is no one there. Hannah follows him into the room, her heart slumping in her chest at the sight of what awaits them. The patio doors have been smashed near the handle, the key lying on the tiled floor. But it is the row of cupboards lining the far wall that she can't take her eyes from. Sprayed across their ivory doors in red paint the colour of fresh blood is the word *LIAR*. It screams at her from across the room like an accusation.

'Oh my God.' Her hand moves to her mouth involuntarily. She scans the room, looking for anything that might be missing, something that might suggest a robbery. Other than a mug that has been knocked from the draining board and has broken into two pieces – one half sitting at the foot of the cupboards, the other resting beside the fridge – everything seems to be in place. Nothing appears to have been taken. 'We need to call the police.'

Michael picks the key up from the floor and locks the doors before moving to the drawer in which the bin bags are kept.

'I took the key out of the lock earlier,' Hannah tells him, hearing her voice falter. 'I took it out before I went upstairs to bed and put it in the box in the hallway.'

Michael looks at her, not needing to speak to make his doubt known.

'Michael, I did, I swear. That key shouldn't be there.'

'Well it is.'

She watches as he tears a bin bag from the roll, followed by another two. He splits their sides so that they are open and then searches the drawer for a roll of masking tape.

'Don't worry about it now,' he says. 'What's done is done.'

'Michael,' Hannah urges, feeling frustrated as she watches him begin to tape the opened bin bags across the hole in the smashed glass. 'We need to call the police.'

'I'll do it,' he says. 'I just want to stop this breeze – it'll be freezing in here in no time.'

The surge of adrenaline racing through Hannah's body has kept her from feeling the cold until now, but as soon as Michael mentions it, she realises he is right. It is late April and though the weather has mostly been kind to them for the past few weeks, tonight it has been raining on and off. If it starts up again, there is nothing to stop driving rain from entering the kitchen and further damage being done.

Night air fills the room, chilling her bare legs. But as her eyes rest again upon the word sprayed across the cupboards, she realises that nothing could be as chilling as those four letters that glare at her.

LIAR.

Which of them does it refer to: her, or him?

Her mind takes her back to the key. She didn't leave it in the back door; she knows she didn't. In her head, she acts out her movements from that evening, repeating them over and over, knowing that she took the key and put it away but watching the memory of it fade until she begins to doubt herself.

'I feel sick,' she says, thinking aloud. She goes to the sink and takes a glass from the draining board before finding a packet of painkillers and swallowing two, seeking respite from the headache that has come from nowhere and filled her skull with its immediate insistency. She watches Michael as he continues taping the bin bags across the door. If the person who was here wishes to return, she thinks, there is little to stop them from doing so.

'How did they get in?'

Michael stops what he is doing and turns to her, his face suggesting that it is a stupid question.

'I don't mean the door,' she says. 'I mean the garden. How did they get into the garden?'

Their house is a fortress, the garden protected by high walls. They designed it when the girls were young, with safety and security in mind. They love their privacy, and they chose this house for its corner plot, away from the neighbours on a quiet cul-de-sac on which break-ins like this never happen. Yet there is a first time for everything, Hannah thinks, and she wonders why it was their house that was targeted.

'Over the wall,' Michael says, finishing his job of blocking out the night air. 'Must have been; there's no other way. Probably teenagers.'

'Plural?'

'Or just the one,' he says, his voice rising. 'I don't know, do I?'

He stands back and observes his handiwork, his face giving away his thoughts. He appears to be thinking the same as Hannah: that a bin bag and a bit of masking tape won't do much to keep out a repeat offender.

'Whoever it was, they won't come back,' he says, giving voice to Hannah's unspoken fears.

'How do you know that?'

'I don't,' he admits. 'It's just very unlikely.'

Hannah stares at the cupboards, the bright red letters staring back. 'Why would a teenager write that?' She could comprehend vandalism, just about, but the word seems so specific and deliberate. A teenager would leave a signature or an expletive, surely, not something that seems aimed at someone for a reason. It makes no sense that someone they don't know would break in at random, take nothing, and leave them with this.

'Will you call the police now?' she asks, when Michael doesn't respond to her question.

Hannah has never made a call to the police in her life, and she doesn't want to start now. They are going to ask what that word on the cupboards might refer to, and what is she supposed to tell them? She has no idea what it means or who it is directed at, yet at the same time it manages to make her feel sick to her stomach. Just knowing that an intruder has been here in her home, in her safe place, is enough to make her scream, which she does inside her own head, silently and where she can control it.

'If I call them now, they're going to come over here tonight,' Michael tells her.

Hannah raises her eyes to the ceiling. That's exactly what they want, isn't it, to get someone over here as soon as possible so they can find out who's responsible. They need to report this – she wants to know who has been here – but she doesn't want the girls knowing more than they need to. It is only as she thinks this that she remembers Olivia on the stairs; she will still be awake, perhaps having listened to their conversation from the landing. Hannah saw her go into her room, but neither of them knows whether she has since come back out.

She goes to the kitchen door and closes it. 'What are we going to tell them?'

'The police?'

'The girls. This will terrify Rosie – she'll have nightmares for weeks.'

'You think it's best they don't know about it?'

'Olivia already knows, though, doesn't she?'

Hannah watches her husband's face carefully, studying his features as they shift and change.

'We don't know how much she knows. Perhaps she didn't see anything. Anyway, she won't tell Rosie, not if we ask her not to.'

She raises an eyebrow. Her husband obviously has greater confidence in their older child than she currently does. She berates herself for the thought, wondering if perhaps she is being unfair on her. Olivia is headstrong and defiant, but she isn't cruel. She never has been – not until recently, at least – and Hannah can't see why she might start to be so now. To her, perhaps, but not to Rosie.

'Where was Olivia?' she asks. 'When you saw her on the stairs, how far down was she? How much would she have seen? The kitchen door was shut, wasn't it? Perhaps you're right; maybe she didn't see anything.'

She can hear herself rambling but can't help it. Her thoughts are spilling from her with the same confusion in which they are entering her head, sporadic and random, catching her off guard.

Michael shakes his head. 'She was halfway down. Whoever was here was already gone.'

His focus moves to the cupboards; Hannah watches him study the sprayed letters, the paint running in tiny streams from each one, like bloodied tears staining a face.

'Why is Olivia refusing to talk to you?' he asks, speaking without looking at her.

Hannah shifts uncomfortably. They've already had this conversation. When he got back from his work trip, she had to explain their daughter's strange behaviour. She couldn't bring herself to tell him the truth – that Olivia had been to the party they had told her she couldn't go to – so she had given an altered version of it: that she was angry about missing out and had fallen silent in protest at them having stopped her.

'She's just being a teenager. She hasn't got her own way and she's letting me know she's not happy about it.'

Michael looks at her now, his eyes wide with an unspoken suggestion.

Hannah waits for a moment, expecting him to say something, and when he doesn't speak, she reads his silent words, refusing to accept them as a possibility. 'No,' she says, with a shake of her head. 'She can't have.'

'Why not?' Michael challenges.

Hannah doesn't have to consider her answer, not when there are a hundred reasons why what he is suggesting is ludicrous. It couldn't possibly have been Olivia who did this. 'She's angry, but she's not malicious.'

'Kids react unpredictably all the time,' Michael says. 'They act on impulse – they don't think things through.'

Hannah shakes her head again. There is no way that her daughter would do this to her. She knows how much she loves that kitchen, and anyway, what would *LIAR* even mean? *BITCH* she might have been able to believe – Olivia would never dare speak the word aloud to her, but Hannah is sure that's what she thinks of her – but *LIAR* has no relevance. It makes no sense.

'Where would she have got spray paint from?' she says weakly, as though this is her only argument for Olivia not being responsible. In truth, there is so much more that doesn't make sense about what Michael is suggesting. The house has been broken into, or appears that way, at least. They saw Olivia and she looked calm; she didn't look like a girl who had just done what Michael obviously thinks her capable of.

Olivia seemed calm, Hannah thinks again, and then the strangeness of that fact occurs to her. If she had heard someone break in and had headed to the staircase at the sound of noise from the kitchen, then why would she seem calm? Why wasn't she panicking? A normal reaction would have been for her to be scared.

She thinks back to last night, and to Olivia arriving home drunk from that party she wasn't supposed to have gone to. She was calm then too.

'She could have got the spray paint during a lunch break,' Michael suggests. For a moment Hannah has forgotten what she asked him, her thoughts having led her down a path she doesn't want to be taken.

'She doesn't leave the school grounds until home time. They're not allowed.'

He pulls a face. 'You think she follows every rule like she's supposed to? Come on, Hannah. We don't know where she is every minute of the day, do we?' His words send a burst of guilt pulsing through her.

'She couldn't have done it,' she says, but she hears the doubt in her own voice.

Michael shifts closer to her and puts a hand on her arm. 'I know you don't want to believe it, love, but there's every possibility she might have. She wasn't in her bed when we got up, and I didn't hear her leave her room, did you?'

She knows he has a point, and the more she allows herself to consider it, the more she realises that there could be some truth in what Michael says. By the time they were woken, Olivia might already have been downstairs. They assumed that she was halfway down the stairs, but what if she was on her way back up? Hannah shakes her head, not wanting to be led any closer to the thoughts her brain is presenting. She doesn't even want to consider the possibility, because if what Michael suggests really is true, then just how out of control have they allowed their daughter to become?

'I don't want to believe it any more than you do,' Michael says, reading her thoughts. 'And perhaps I'm wrong; I hope to God I am. Maybe I'm being unfair to even think it. It could have been anyone – someone drunk or high on drugs, someone who got the wrong house, even.'

He puts his arm around her and pulls her closer to him, wrapping her in an embrace. Hannah rests her head on his shoulder, inhaling the familiar scent of his aftershave. She feels better already just for being next to him, and now she feels guilty about what happened earlier, for not showing him the enthusiasm she knows he deserves.

'Let's not worry about this mess tonight,' he says. 'We'll sort it out in the morning.'

Hannah shakes her head. 'I don't want Rosie to see it.' As soon as she says it, she realises she is already considering Olivia as a suspect. She knows she should probably feel ashamed to even think it of her own daughter – after all, if Olivia is capable of this, then what does that say about her as a mother? – but she cannot help herself.

'Why smash the door, though?' she asks, clinging on to the hope that Olivia is innocent.

'To make it look like a break-in. Look,' he says, holding her by the arms and moving back from her, 'do you still want me to call the police? I'll do it if you really want me to, but if anything points towards Liv, then we're not going to be able to protect her. If she's involved, they'll find out. I hope to God she's not, love, I really do, but once they pick up on something, they'll want to know what's been going on here, about this argument and everything. She'll have a record for life, and if they think she's out of control in some way, we'll end up with social services involved.'

Hannah exhales loudly, knowing that everything he says is right. She moves back into his arms, easing her chest against the warmth of him as he rubs her back through her nightdress.

'I'm so sorry, Han,' he says gently. 'I hope I'm wrong, but we need to be sure first, don't we?'

She nods, but says nothing.

'There's some gloss in the garage,' he says. 'I'll paint over the damage. The girls might not notice, and if they do, I'll think of something.' He leans down and kisses her forehead. 'Go and get some sleep.'

She nods again, but knows she won't go back upstairs, not until he's ready to go up with her. She doesn't want to get back into bed alone; as well as that, she doesn't want to risk seeing Olivia. The thought that she might be responsible for this lodges itself in her brain, refusing to be budged by any reasoning or doubt. The look on her daughter's face when they saw her on the staircase has set itself in stone in her mind, the expression so distant and yet so filled with something else. Smug, Hannah thinks. She doesn't want to admit it even to herself, but Olivia looked smug at the sight of her parents' panic.

'I'll be back in a minute,' Michael says, unlocking the patio doors to go out to the garage.

'Be careful.'

When he's gone, Hannah stands in front of the cupboards, the word *LIAR* screaming at her with a silent accusation that manages to pierce her eardrums with its noise. She studies the red streaks, like blood dripping down the cupboard doors. The choice of colour wasn't an accident, she knows that, but what exactly is somebody trying to tell her?

If Olivia has done this, Hannah thinks, then she has never really known her own daughter at all.

And if her daughter thinks she's a liar, just what does she think she's lied about?

FOUR

OLIVIA

When Olivia goes downstairs the following morning, her father is sitting at the kitchen table. He doesn't so much as turn his head to acknowledge her as she enters the room. The kitchen smells of paint. Will he mention what happened here last night? she wonders. Will her mother?

This kitchen is her mother's pride and joy. Olivia can just about recall what the house was like years ago, before the extension was built. She has memories of noisy builders and loud music played from a radio that was always crackly, and her mother being in a state of constant stress; she was pregnant with Rosie at the time, and the work was completed during a sticky summer in which all Olivia can recollect of her mother is a huge stomach and a red, flustered face.

If Olivia wasn't so hungry, she wouldn't have come downstairs, but it is Sunday now, and she hasn't eaten anything since before the party on Friday night. She lay in bed listening to her stomach rumble for an hour after waking up, by which time she was forced to admit to herself that she was going to have to go downstairs and face whatever awaited her there. The silence that greeted her was not at all what she expected. They are playing her at her own game, though she isn't sure what they expect to achieve by it.

She pours herself a bowl of cereal and takes the milk from the fridge. She can feel her father's eyes on her back as she prepares her breakfast, but she won't be unnerved by him. After what happened last night, it should be he and her mother feeling unnerved.

She takes her cereal outside and sits on the patio slabs. Rosie is curled in on herself at the foot of the tree at the end of the garden, her willowy frame like that of a woodland fairy. Whenever she can't be found inside the house, there's only one other place she is likely to be: sitting beneath this tree, her legs crossed, her head bowed over the pages of the latest book she has borrowed from the school library, her red hair drawing a curtain around her that shuts her off from the world. She seems to think it makes her superior; that she knows more for having spent so many hours of her young life immersed in make-believe, but Olivia thinks the opposite is true. While Rosie is lost in stories, she doesn't see what's going on in the real world, what's happening right in front of her. Olivia feels sorry for her. When the truth of what their parents are hits her, Rosie won't have been expecting a thing.

Their mother appears from the patio doors carrying a basket of washing that has just been pulled from the machine. She casts Olivia a glance but does not allow the look to linger, instead resting the basket on the table outside while she sets about lowering the washing line. Olivia wonders why she is bothering; the sky is still grey and heavy from last night's rain and looks as though it is ready to burst open with a downpour.

'Would you like a drink?' her mother asks, directing the question at the washing line.

It takes Olivia a moment to realise that her mother is talking to her. She finds her calmness unnerving. Her mother has never been prone to verbal outbursts or bouts of anger; placidity is ingrained within her, a taught behaviour. Olivia is nothing like her, not in looks or in temperament. Her mother is tall and copper-haired like Rosie; Olivia is shorter, heavier, brunette. If she was able to scream and shout – if she could tell her mother in one long frustration-fuelled rant exactly what she thinks of her – Olivia knows she would revel in doing so, that it would be exactly the kind of outburst her mother avoids. As things are, she must say nothing and just bite her tongue; wait for her mother to do something that will shatter the invisible glass that has been placed between them.

Olivia spent the previous day reminding herself that she wasn't to reply when either of her parents spoke to her. It took a surprising amount of concentration to remember not to speak, but already it feels so much easier. She thinks her mother will leave her alone now, but she doesn't; instead, she abandons her task of hanging out the washing and goes over to Olivia, squatting on her heels to join her near the ground.

'I don't know whether your father has said anything to you,' she says quietly, her face close to Olivia's, 'but you do not mention anything about last night to Rosie. Understood?'

She waits; she won't leave without some form of response. She is too close, close enough that Olivia inhales the sickly-sweet perfume that her mother has sprayed on her throat. Her make-up has been applied; she can see the evidence of foundation in the lines at her eyes and around the corners of her mouth. Regardless of everything that has happened, the mask is back in place and the show must go on.

Her mother is not going to get up until Olivia has offered an acknowledgement of her words, and so she nods, the most she is going to offer her.

'Whatever you think of me,' her mother continues, 'Rosie hasn't done anything. I don't want her being upset or frightened by anything.' She stands and leaves.

Olivia finishes her cereal, then takes her bowl into the kitchen. As she washes it, dries it and replaces it in the cupboard, she feels her father watching her again. She waits for him to speak, but he says nothing. She goes back outside and heads to the end of the garden to sit with Rosie. When she turns back to the house, her mother is at the patio doors watching her, her face as bleak as the skies above them, darkened with a silent warning, the kind that Olivia has seen so many times before. Olivia holds her stare, trying to keep her expression as vacant and as difficult to read as she can.

'What do you want?' Rosie asks, not looking up from the pages of her book.

'Charming,' Olivia mumbles.

'Oh ... you're talking to me, then?'

'Why wouldn't I be?'

'Well, you're not speaking to Mum and Dad, are you? I heard them talking about it earlier.'

'You shouldn't eavesdrop. What were they saying?'

Rosie tuts. 'If I wasn't supposed to be listening, I shouldn't really repeat it to you, should I?'

'Rosie,' Olivia hisses through gritted teeth. She sighs and puts a hand on her sister's knee. 'I'm sorry,' she says, regretting taking her frustration out on her.

'It's fine.' Rosie is wearing black leggings that manage to make her stick legs look even thinner than they are. 'They were just saying you were going through a phase, that's all. That it'll all blow over soon enough.'

Olivia shakes her head; that is typical of her parents, she thinks.

'You're just like Dorothy,' Rosie says ambiguously.

Olivia rolls her eyes and removes her hand from Rosie's leg. 'Who's Dorothy?'

'In *The Wizard of Oz*. Mum's always saying how restless you get. But just remember, Olivia ...' Rosie raises her hands and makes inverted comma marks with her fingers, the gesture managing to irritate her sister more than she could have anticipated, 'there's no place like home.' She taps her heels together and gives Olivia a look that lingers longer than feels normal, some silent communication passed between them. Then her smile fades to a frown, and Olivia knows what she is saying. She knows that Rosie understands. She smiles sadly, but Rosie has already returned her focus to her book.

Olivia glances back at the house, thinking that Rosie's statement couldn't be further from the truth. And yet perhaps in some ways she is right. Maybe there really is no other place like this one.

'You didn't hear anything last night then?'

Rosie doesn't look up from her book. 'No. Why, what happened last night?'

'I don't know. Something's happened to the back door, though.'

'Oh, that. Mum said Dad was moving furniture or something.'

Olivia looks at her sister with disbelief, but Rosie still doesn't look up from her book. She can't be this naïve, can she? Or is it easier there, in Rosie's own little made-up world, ignoring the things that are going on around her?

'What are you reading, anyway?' Olivia reaches for Rosie's book, ignoring her cry of protest. '*A Dog's Life*,' she says, looking at the cartoon on the cover. 'Bit babyish, isn't it?'

Rosie snatches the book back and gives a smug smile. 'I'm enjoying it,' she says, returning to her page. 'It's very educational, actually.'

Olivia narrows her eyes. She shifts on the grass and looks over Rosie's shoulder, her eyes darting to the top of the page. *The Boyfriend* is typed in the header. She scans lower: *He was everything she had been dreaming about and more … He threw stones at her window, waking her from her sleep … It didn't matter that it was dark; when they kissed, a million stars lit up the sky above them …*

'Give that here,' she says, taking the book back and pulling off the dust cover. She smiles at what lies beneath it, impressed by Rosie's cunning. Perhaps her sister isn't so daft after all.

Rosie smirks, proud of herself and the way she's managed to fool their mother, then takes the book back and wraps the *Dog's*

Life cover around it again. 'How long are you going to keep this up, then?'

'Keep what up?'

'Mum and Dad. When are you planning on talking to them again?'

'I'm not.' Olivia stretches her legs out in front of her. She's wearing jeans and a jumper, but she still feels cold. She wishes it was warmer.

Rosie shuffles her bum to sit alongside her, copying her position by placing her legs alongside her sister's. 'I'm almost as tall as you,' she says, tapping her left foot against Olivia's ankle.

'No you're not. We're sitting down; it doesn't work like that.'

'Why won't you speak to them?' Rosie asks, refusing to let the subject drop.

'It's complicated.'

'*You're* complicated, you mean.'

'You don't get it,' Olivia says, moving her sister's legs away from her so that they're no longer touching. 'You think you're smart, but you don't get anything.'

'I get that you don't do what you're told,' Rosie says, and there is something so annoyingly smug in her tone that Olivia feels like ripping the book from her hands and tearing out the pages. She wouldn't, though. No matter how infuriating her little sister is at times, Olivia hates it when Rosie cries. She is the best friend she has – the only friend she has – and she wishes they were closer in age, that they had more in common they could share with each other.

She pushes herself back along the grass and sits up, crossing her legs beneath her. 'Neither do you, by the looks of things,' she says with a smile, gesturing to the book. 'And is that what we're supposed to do? Just do as we're told?'

Rosie scrunches her mouth and looks up to the sky as she considers her answer. A mass of black clouds is rolling towards them from the east, chilling the air that circles them. 'We're just kids. So I suppose so, yeah.'

'No,' Olivia corrects her. 'You're just a kid. I'm fifteen. In a few months I'll be able to leave home. I could get married if I wanted to.'

'No you couldn't,' Rosie says, taking obvious pleasure in the opportunity to correct her. 'You'd have to have Mum and Dad's permission. Unless you went to Scotland. I think you can get married there at sixteen. But you don't even have a boyfriend, so I don't suppose you'll be getting married any time soon, will you? You can borrow this after me, if you like,' she adds, waving the book in the air. 'Maybe you'll pick up some tips.'

Olivia grits her teeth, trying to push back the irritation that Rosie so often manages to spark in her. She can be so annoying, always having to prove herself right, taking enjoyment from making her older sister look small and stupid. Everyone in the house does this to her. Olivia feels like an outsider here. She always has.

As though sensing her thoughts, Rosie reaches for Olivia's hand. 'You won't go anywhere, will you?'

Olivia looks down at their interlocking fingers, wondering why Rosie goes out of her way to annoy her when they so obviously need each other.

'Of course I won't.' And despite everything she feels about this place – despite the fragility that holds their life here together – she knows this is one promise she can make with certainty.

Dear Diary,

I have met a boy. Well, not a boy, actually – he's a man. He is handsome and funny and generous. I can't stop thinking about him. Mum would kill me if she found out I'd been talking to him, but if I do things the right way, then she never has to know. It will be like living a double life – how exciting is that?! I wonder how long I can get away with it. I'm glad I can tell you about him – there's no one else to talk to. I wish I had a friend, a female friend, someone I could share my secrets with, but it doesn't seem to matter so much now. I'm not alone any more. He loves me and I love him. He might be able to help me escape this place, but in the meantime, he can stay our secret, just you and me.

FIVE

HANNAH

On Monday morning, Hannah walks the girls to school as usual. Rosie's primary school is closer to home than the comprehensive Olivia attends, and when they near the gates, her younger daughter turns and kisses her mother dutifully before hurrying to the main doors. Olivia's school is a few streets further away, and she and Hannah complete the walk in a silence that is becoming unsettlingly familiar. Olivia hasn't uttered a word to either of her parents since Friday evening. Despite her wishes for the phone to remain confiscated, Michael insisted upon Hannah returning it to Olivia, but not even that could prompt a response. The silence is scaring Hannah, smothering her as though it might suffocate her.

'Have a good day,' she says, as they turn a corner and the building looms ahead of them.

Olivia shoves her bag further up her shoulder and says nothing, almost colliding with a woman as she storms off towards the school.

'I'm sorry,' Hannah says, apologising for the awkwardness left by her daughter's poor manners.

'Teenagers,' the woman says with a smile. 'Mine's only in year eight, but you'd think he's seventeen the way he carries on.'

Hannah gives the woman a small smile. She doesn't want to get trapped into a conversation with this stranger, yet she doesn't want to go home to an empty house either.

'How old's yours?' the woman asks.

'Fifteen, going on thirty. Knows it all already.'

'Sounds familiar,' the woman says, rolling her eyes. 'When they're babies, people tell you it gets easier, don't they? They really shouldn't lie about it.'

Hannah laughs. She is surprised at the sound; a sound she realises she hasn't heard in a long time.

'Anyway, got to go,' the woman says with an apologetic shrug of the shoulders. 'I'll be late for work at this rate. See you again.'

'Bye.'

The woman presses a key fob, and the lights flash on a car parked at the other side of the road. Hannah watches her for a moment as she crosses the road and gets into the car, and finds herself wondering where this woman works and what her life might look like beyond just being a mum. The thought that perhaps it would have been nice to talk a little longer crosses her mind, but it leaves her as quickly as it arrived, replaced with reminders of all the menial jobs she needs to get done that day, and the thought that the kind of life involving meeting for coffee and small talk belongs to other people.

Michael always leaves the house by 7.30 on weekdays, and by 9 a.m. Hannah is back home, the rest of the day stretching out in front of her. Some days, these school hours pass quickly, her time filled with household chores and garden maintenance. She takes a pride in her home, and there is always something to be done: clothes to be ironed and put away, surfaces to be dusted, windows to be cleaned. She has never been religious, yet she understands the idea of cleanliness being next to godliness. She couldn't live a life of disarray; it would simply cause her too much stress. She likes things to be structured and orderly; she likes to know where things are so that they can be easily located.

Saturday night's break-in preyed on her mind throughout Sunday, and it continues to do so now. She doesn't want to believe that Olivia could be responsible for what happened here, in their own house, and yet so much of what her husband says makes sense, as unsettling as that sense might be. She feels violated by the attack on her home and has contemplated going to the police, yet the thought of her daughter being involved has stopped her. This is the hardest part, the bitterest pill to swallow, because Hannah realises that if she is holding back for this reason, then deep in her heart she must believe Olivia is guilty.

She goes into her daughter's bedroom and stands in the doorway, surveying it as though it is unfamiliar territory to her and not a room she has entered for every day of her daughter's almost-sixteen years of life. As children, both girls were taught to tidy up after themselves, but in recent months Olivia seems to have forgotten all she knows about acceptable behaviour. Yesterday's clothes have been thrown on the carpet at the foot of the bed, which has been left unmade. Dirty cups litter the bedside table; a tea ring stains the wood. It seems that she is intent on doing everything she can to defy her parents' wishes.

Swallowing down a lump of frustration at her daughter's disrespect and ingratitude, Hannah goes to the wardrobe. Inside, Olivia's clothes are hung up neatly, the items ordered in categories – jeans, T-shirts, jumpers – as though she doesn't mind being organised in places where it can't be witnessed by anyone else. She crouches and pushes aside the shoes that line the bottom of the wardrobe. She knows what she is looking for; it is simply a matter of finding it.

The thought that her daughter might be hiding the can of spray paint used to graffiti the kitchen cupboards makes her feel sick with a combination of anger and disappointment. Of course, she knew that Olivia's teenage years would present the family with testing times – it would have been naïve to hope for anything else – but searching her bedroom for spray paint isn't something she has ever envisioned herself having to do, and she can't escape the feeling of failure that has swamped her since Saturday night. It could be worse, she thinks wearily. She realises that some of the kids Olivia's age are up to all sorts, things she is probably unable to imagine. They say that parents can't be blamed for everything their child does, but Hannah doesn't really agree. Why don't these people know where their children are and what they're doing? It is their responsibility to raise them to be good, decent human beings. It is their duty to protect them.

When the wardrobe offers her nothing, Hannah checks above and below it. She is careful to leave everything as it was when she entered the room, not wanting Olivia to know that she has been in here. It occurs to her that her daughter's outrage at knowing her mother has been through her things might be enough to force her into speaking, but it would only lead to another argument, and she isn't ready for that, not yet. If silence means peace for the time being at least, then that is how she will allow things to remain. For now, anyway. She needs time to think, to consider what needs to be done for the best, for the sake of everyone's happiness and well-being.

The bedside drawers don't hold very much, and it doesn't take her long to look through their contents. She removes a couple of school reports, a packet of hair grips and a hairbrush, a small album filled with photographs of Olivia and Rosie when they were younger, most of them taken outside in the garden. She pauses her search to look through the photographs, lingering on how young the girls look in each image and how different things were back then, when they were all games and innocence. It wasn't that long ago really – six, seven years at most – and yet nothing seems as it was, just that short space of time enough to turn everything upside down.

Closing the photograph album, Hannah sits for a moment in silence, bathing in the past that lingers invisible in the air around her. She remembers this room as it once was: the pink bed with a white canopy hanging from the ceiling, flocks of flying fairies circling the walls; sequinned curtains that would shimmer in the soft glow of the bedside lamp. She spent hours in this room with Olivia when she was young, whole afternoons role-playing and creating classrooms with the soft toys, which they would line up against the wall and read to. If she focuses enough, she can see their shadows still playing. Her visits here are now restricted to waking Olivia up when she doesn't want to scrape herself from beneath her duvet, or checking that she hasn't left the room in a state that might be regarded a health hazard.

She stands from the bed and forces herself from her thoughts. She scans the room, remembering that she is here for a purpose and that she can't leave until she has found what she's looking for. Think, Hannah, she tells herself. She remembers what it was to be fifteen, to keep things from her mother. If she was a teenager, where would she keep her darkest secrets? She kneels on the carpet and gropes under the bed. She lowers her head and puts her ear to the floor, craning her neck to look up at the slats. She knows it is unlikely that a can of spray paint could be wedged beneath a mattress, but there is something else waiting here for her. She pulls it out and looks at it, her thumb tracing the edge of the diary.

Back on her feet, her heart pounding, she looks at the clock, remembering that it is Monday and that she needs to be somewhere by midday. It's the same routine every week; it has been like this for quite some time now. She leaves the house by 11.40 and makes the twenty-minute walk to the care home, the route now so familiar to her she could find the place with her eyes closed. She spends an hour there with her mother before returning home, back at the house by 1.30 p.m. It is a part of the shape of her life now, and she wonders how long it might continue.

She goes into her bedroom and puts the diary on top of the wardrobe. She will need to find a better hiding place for it when she gets back this afternoon, but she doesn't have time now and she doesn't want to be late. No one will be home before she is, so there's no chance of anyone else getting their hands on it before she has an opportunity to move it.

Heading back downstairs, she takes her coat from the end of the banister and reaches for the handle of the front door. Her keys aren't in the lock. She is sure she left them there when she got home earlier; now, the door is locked as she left it, but the keys are gone. She realises the extent to which the events of the weekend have affected her. She hasn't felt right since Friday, since Olivia snuck out of the house and the argument that followed. The atmosphere has changed; something has shifted and come undone. Her daughter's silence has filled the house, sitting amongst them with the threat of worse to come. There is an unravelling that Hannah fears cannot be tied back up to keep the fabric of their family together.

There is a box screwed to the hallway wall near the front door where she and Michael keep their keys, but when Hannah checks it now, it is empty. She searches through the pockets of her coat before going into the kitchen, thinking that maybe she made a mistake and took the keys there earlier. She looks everywhere she can think of, even checking inside the microwave and the fridge – she can't dismiss the idea that she might have absent-mindedly left them in such a place. She has been so distracted by everything that has been going on that nothing would surprise her.

When she can't find them, frustration grips her. She thinks about calling Michael, but she doesn't want to disturb him at work with something so clumsy and trivial. After everything else that has happened during these past few days, a phone call from home might trigger an unwarranted panic, something Hannah doesn't want to be responsible for. He already has so many other things to worry about.

It is now gone midday; she is already late, and even if she was able to leave now, she wouldn't get there for another twenty minutes. Resigning herself to the fact that today's visit won't happen, she goes to the house phone and dials the number that has been used so often in recent months it's now stored in her head.

'It's Hannah Walters,' she says when the call to the home is answered. 'Yes, that's right ... Can you tell her I won't be there today? Yes ... sorry. Thanks.'

She hangs up knowing she should feel worse about not being able to visit her mother. The truth is, she doesn't feel that bad at all. If she's honest with herself, not being able to go has come as a relief. Rather than tormenting herself with thoughts of a guilt she just can't conjure up, she flicks the switch on the kettle. The room still smells of paint, and what happened here on Saturday cannot be escaped, no matter how desperately she tries to shut it out.

The idea of an intruder standing here, just feet from where she is now, distracts her momentarily from thoughts of anything else. The image in her brain shifts and distorts, so that the shadowed stranger she sees in her imagination is replaced by Olivia, an alien and quietly satisfied look of victory on her face. Hannah sees her lips move; hears the word 'liar' as her daughter fades and disappears.

Feeling nausea roll in her stomach, she makes herself a cup of tea she won't drink and sits at the kitchen table, trying to empty her mind of the thoughts that linger there and the image of Olivia that returns unbidden. She watches her at the cupboards, armed with a can of spray paint, her resentment escaping her as she scrawls the word *LIAR* in a shock of blood red. The word is so specific, so intentional. Just how much does Olivia know?

As Hannah wonders what her daughter might have found out about her, the girl who isn't really at the other side of the kitchen turns slowly. She looked like Olivia from behind, but face on, her features are different and her clothes have changed, the jeans and T-shirt combination that has become her unofficial uniform replaced by a dress that is too short, and torn at the front. There are bruises on her bare arms. There is blood on her face.

Hannah closes her eyes and puts her head in her hands, her elbows resting on the kitchen table. She begins to hum, a tuneless, droning noise that attempts to drown out the other sounds filling her head. On any other Monday, being stuck inside the house would come as something to be welcomed, but now, after what has happened over the weekend and the ghosts it has left her with, she wants to be anywhere else. The safe place that was once her home doesn't feel so safe any more.

SIX

OLIVIA

The thought of going to school that morning makes Olivia feel sick. Usually, no matter how bad things are there, school is a more appealing option than home. They walk in silence, the air yet again thick and heavy with the threat of rain, the last of the warm spring days behind them for the time being. Olivia leaves her mother at the usual corner, already feeling her schoolmates' stares burning through her skin. She wonders what might have been said about her since Friday night, then asks herself whether she really cares. The answer, of course, is that she does. She wants to fit in with these people. She needs to believe she can fit in somewhere.

By third lesson, she hopes that the worst of what might have been said has already come and gone. She heard a couple of comments passed between the girls sitting behind her during registration; she knows she heard the word *skank*, though she pretended not to notice that they were talking about her. The truth is, the word cut into her chest, piercing her heart with a violence that felt physical. She tries to tell herself it doesn't hurt, that she can't feel the pain, but it does and she can, and it all feels like a whole new rejection, just another to add to the list of knock-backs that have passed before it.

Thinking about what happened at that party on Friday night makes her face flush with colour, yet she knows that if she could go back and restart the weekend – if she could go to that party again knowing what would be said and how she would feel afterwards –

she would do it all again, exactly the same. Perhaps what she did was wrong – she knows it probably was. But Olivia is sick of being told what is right. She wants to find out for herself.

English is third lesson, and she takes her usual place near the front, by a window that overlooks the staff car park. She sits next to the other class oddball, a girl called Manon who is new to the school and who no one really bothers with. Olivia empathises with her, but she doesn't want to be her friend. If she gets too close to the new girl she will only alienate herself even further from everyone else. When you're already strange, she thinks, you don't need the help of other weirdos to make you even odder.

They are asked to get out their homework, which she finally managed to complete while still in bed on Saturday, a welcome distraction from the headache and the regret that otherwise consumed her. They have been studying *Of Mice and Men* in preparation for their exam. It is bleak and depressing, and Olivia doesn't want to believe any more that bleak and depressing are all that life has to offer. There must be something else.

'Who'd like to start us off?' Miss Johnson asks. She smiles and glances from row to row, waiting for one of the students to volunteer. Monday's English lessons always begin in the same way, with the sharing of homework and the inevitable silence that falls as every member of the class tries to avoid drawing unwanted attention to themselves. Miss Johnson says it's an opportunity to learn from each other, but Olivia has yet to work out what might be learned from some of the people in the class.

'Aaron,' Miss Johnson says, resting her eyes on one of the boys in the back row. 'I assume that's your homework you're studying so intently there?'

Aaron slides his phone from his lap, puts it back into his pocket and rolls his eyes. Miss Johnson never seems to get too much backchat, even from the kids who play up during other teachers' lessons. She is well respected even though she's young, still in her twenties, and Olivia guesses it's because most of the boys fancy her. She is pretty, and she doesn't talk to them as though they're still in primary school like a lot of the other teachers do. Olivia likes her, though she doesn't want to show it too much.

'Actually,' Aaron says, 'I have done it.' He flips through his exercise book and finds the homework. 'Which bit do you want?'

'How much have you written?'

He holds the book up; he has written little more than a paragraph, and even that has been scrawled in the biggest writing it seems he was able to manage. Miss Johnson raises an eyebrow. 'Won't even get you a pass in the exam,' she tells him. 'Doesn't even matter what you've written – it's not enough. Come on, you know you need to write more than that.' She sighs. 'Read it to us then.'

Aaron clears his throat as though he's about to deliver a sermon. 'Curley's wife doesn't have a name because she is only known as her husband's property. This shows how women were treated as objects and didn't have their own identity. She flirts with the men on the ranch for attention and she does it to wind Curley up, which always works. The other men think she is trouble and they're right because everything that happens in the book is her fault and if she hadn't messed with Lennie then neither of them would of ended up dead.'

He looks up from his book, pleased with his efforts.

'Okay,' Miss Johnson says. 'There's the start of some good points there, Aaron. You're going to need quotations in the exam, though. When you write that the other men think she's trouble—'

'Jailbait,' someone calls out, cutting her short.

'Exactly. An easy one to remember. What do we think, then?'

She waits for someone to offer their thoughts on Aaron's homework, but no one speaks. Next to Olivia, Manon shifts uncomfortably in her chair, her head kept lowered to the table. Olivia can feel the girl's anxiety pulsing from her in waves, static in the air between them, and she feels a sympathy for her that she isn't sure anyone else in this room could be capable of.

'Aaron says that Curley's wife flirts with the men on the ranch for attention,' Miss Johnson says, trying to prompt the class. 'Is he right?'

'Yeah.'

'What do we make of her behaviour, then?' She waits before directing the question at another of the boys in Aaron's row.

'Well,' he says, 'she's a bit of a slag really, isn't she?'

There are a few titters among the students. Olivia feels her own anxiety heighten, as though she and Manon are now encased in the same bubble of awkwardness that separates them from the rest of the class.

'Not the nicest way of phrasing it,' Miss Johnson says, 'but some people may see her like that. There's a reason for most things, though. What motivates her behaviour? She must realise that people view her in this way, so why does she do the things she does?'

There is a silence that Olivia feels like a weight pressing down on her, almost as though she knows where this is going and what will happen next. The bubble is closing in around her, stealing her air. She can feel eyes already resting upon her, burning her with the shame that rises in her chest and settles at her throat.

'Ask Olivia,' Joel Murray pipes up from the far corner of the room. 'She'll be able to explain it to you.'

The room is split with the laughter of some and the questioning silence of others. Olivia realises that most of them know what happened on Friday night; gossip spreads through the school quicker than chickenpox at a nursery. She hasn't seen the boy that morning; she doesn't even know whether he's in school. He's in the sixth form, so he might not be here yet; she knows that sometimes they don't bother coming in until their lessons start. She feels her face burn with shame and embarrassment.

When Miss Johnson speaks, her voice is uncharacteristically icy and her tone throws the classroom back into silence. 'Go outside, please, Joel.'

'What?'

'Outside,' Miss Johnson repeats, staring at him with a look that says she is not to be pushed any further.

Joel shoves his chair back, mumbles something and lollops from the classroom with all the grace of a skinny sloth, slamming the door behind him.

'Anyone have anything intelligent to add to the conversation?' Miss Johnson asks. 'Why does Curley's wife behave the way she does?'

'I think it's a cry for help,' Sarah Mayhew says.

'Thank you, Sarah. Go on.'

'Well,' the girl says, glancing over at Olivia, 'she might not be doing it in the best way, but it's like she's just trying to get someone to notice her. Curley neglects her, so she's looking for attention somewhere else. It's not her fault really, is it?'

Miss Johnson smiles, as though grateful that she has finally received a sensible response. 'Exactly. We might not agree with everything she does, but Curley's wife is a character we should feel sympathy for. She's a victim of her husband's abuse, a victim of society's treatment of women, a victim of a failed American Dream. So with that in mind, please, I'd like you all to add to your homework any of the points that have just been raised that you've not already got, and when you've done that, I'd like you to make a start on the extract question I gave you last week.'

She waits for the class to settle into their work before going outside to speak to Joel. Olivia watches as she closes the door behind her, careful to keep the conversation from the ears of the class. Through the glass she sees Joel standing with his head lowered and his hands shoved into his pockets; whatever it is Miss Johnson is saying to him is clearly passing over his head unheeded.

When they return, he heads straight to his seat without making eye contact with Olivia, and Miss Johnson continues the lesson as though nothing happened.

Olivia wills the rest of the hour away, grateful for the sound of the teacher's voice telling them to pack away their things and leave their books on the desk to be collected for marking. She is one of the last to head towards the door, but Miss Johnson stops her.

'Are you okay, Olivia?' she asks.

'Fine,' she says without looking up.

'What happened back then with Joel—' the teacher begins.

'I said I'm fine,' Olivia snaps, throwing her bag onto her shoulder. 'Just leave it, all right.' She hurries out of the classroom, bumping into another student in the corridor.

She spends lunchtime in the library, pretending to read a book she hasn't even looked at the title of. Her stomach rumbles with hunger, but she doesn't want to eat; she can't face the stodgy sandwiches her mother has made her, and she doesn't have any money to buy something from the canteen. She never thought she would find herself feeling this way, but all she wants is for three o'clock to arrive so that she can go home.

When it eventually does – the afternoon having passed without further event – Olivia walks her usual route home. She usually meets her mother and Rosie along the way, but that day there is no sign of either of them. She doesn't wait; despite her hatred of the place, all she wants to do is get back to the house. When she turns into the cul-de-sac on which her family lives, she is stopped by a young woman standing at the entrance to the street. She has a child with her, a small olive-skinned boy of about four or five years old, who grips the woman's hand as he looks at Olivia through a curtain of dark fringe.

'Excuse me,' she says, giving Olivia a small smile. 'Have you got the time, please?'

Olivia gropes in her pocket for her mobile phone, presses the lock key and tells the woman the time that lights up on its screen. The woman is staring at her as she does so; Olivia can feel her eyes fixed to her face, her attention unnerving.

'Thank you,' the woman says, and then, nervously, as though she feels it necessary to break the silence, she adds, 'We're just waiting for someone.'

Olivia smiles awkwardly, but says nothing. As she heads along the pavement, she glances back; the woman is still there, her eyes following her. The little boy is tugging at her arm impatiently, apparently fed up with waiting around.

Olivia gets back to a silent house. Her mother is home – she is always home – but she is in the living room and doesn't come out into the hallway even when she hears Olivia walk through the front door. Olivia catches a glimpse of her as she heads up the stairs; her mother is sitting on the sofa with her back to the living room door, inert as a shop mannequin.

She goes straight to her room and changes out of her uniform, feeling cleaner for just being free of it. She is folding her clothes and placing them in a pile on the chair by the window when she notices the photo album on the bed. It has been in the drawer of her bedside table for years, and Olivia can't remember the last time she looked at it. Her mother has been in her room. This is nothing unusual – there is no privacy in this house, not that she's aware of anyway – but it isn't common for her mother to go through her drawers. If she brings up clothes, she usually leaves them on the bed and tells Olivia to put them away.

Leaving her uniform half folded, Olivia goes to the bed, sits down and pulls open the drawer of the bedside table. She rummages frantically, trying to recall the details of what might have been in there and what her mother might have seen. Then her heart stutters in her chest as she remembers what else was in her room, and she drops from the bed onto the carpet. She looks under the mattress, frantically groping along the slats of the wooden bed frame, but what she's searching for isn't there. The diary has gone. Her mother has taken it.

SEVEN

HANNAH

At some point during the afternoon, Hannah fell asleep on the bed. It isn't like her to do that; she can never usually sleep during the day unless she's unwell, which she knows she's not. Not physically, at least. Mentally, she isn't so sure. She feels exhausted by everything, run down by the erratic journey her thoughts keep taking her on. She wakes up on top of the duvet fully dressed, feeling cold and sick, panicking even though she isn't sure why. It is nearly three o'clock; she will be late for the girls.

As she heads downstairs, the first thing she notices is the open key box by the front door. She left it closed earlier, she knows she did. Her pace quickens down the last few steps and she snatches at the little door of the box, yanking it fully open. Her set of keys is hanging on one of the hooks inside. She takes them out and turns them in her hand, studying them as though there is some sort of mistake and they are not really hers. But they are. And they have been here all day, they must have been. Only Hannah knows they weren't.

She goes into the living room and sits in silence, the keys still in her hand. She should leave now, even though she's already late, but something keeps her rooted to the sofa, too mentally exhausted to move. She trusts Rosie to walk home from school alone just this once, and knows there won't be a problem with her doing so; it is Olivia who worries her. After everything else, she hopes her daughter won't be foolish enough to do anything reckless.

Olivia arrives home from school earlier than Rosie, which Hannah isn't expecting. She doesn't need to go out into the hall to know that it is Olivia; she can tell from the way she clatters in through the front door and almost falls up the stairs, going straight to her room to get changed out of her uniform. Moments later, Rosie appears.

'I'm sorry,' she splutters breathlessly. 'I forgot my homework diary – I had to go back for it.' She stands at the living room door with a sheepish look on her face. 'Where were you? I waited for you for ages.'

'Something came up.' Hannah shrugs the question away. She doesn't mind Rosie's lateness; she is too preoccupied with thoughts of Olivia's silence to worry about much else. 'How was your day?' she asks, her mind still distracted.

'Okay. We made a collage – do you want to see?'

She nods as Rosie comes into the living room and drops her school bag from her shoulder, unzipping it to find the masterpiece she has created. It is too big for the bag and has been folded in half, an impressive array of leaves and twigs glued to a sheet of thin cardboard. Rosie looks at her mother and back at the artwork, turning it to a better angle. 'It's a bird,' she says, her voice hopeful.

'Of course it is,' Hannah says, pulling herself from thoughts of Olivia. She points at each of the bird's features and names them in turn: a beak, a wing, two clawed feet. 'It's lovely, Rosie.'

Rosie smiles half-heartedly, as though accepting her mother's lack of enthusiasm as expected. She packs the bird back into her bag. 'I'm going to get changed.'

Hannah nods, but says nothing as Rosie leaves the room. There is something she needs to do, something she should have done on Sunday.

She goes upstairs to Olivia's room. Her older daughter is sitting on her bed, changed from her school uniform into her pyjamas, a pair with tiny rainbows dotted over the trousers that make her look far younger than she is. She doesn't appear to be doing anything, which makes Hannah suspicious of what she might be hiding.

'Good day at school?' she asks, closing the bedroom door behind her.

Olivia looks at her with a mixture of resentment and anticipation, unsure of what is going on or what is about to happen. There is no response. Hannah didn't expect one, but she wonders just how long Olivia can keep up this silent protest. 'Your father should be home soon,' she continues, glancing at the clock on Olivia's bedroom wall.

Michael is late, but this isn't uncommon. His job seems to involve increasingly long hours, and she knows she can't complain. The money he makes is good; it has paid for their beautiful home and it allows her the freedom not to have to work, a freedom for which she is eternally grateful. The only job she has ever had was as a shop assistant, part-time, when she was a teenager. Though she sometimes wonders what it might be like to have a career, she has no regrets about the choices she has made. Having a family at such a young age might never have been on her agenda, but she knows that her life is everything she ever wanted, and during her hardest days she reminds herself of the fact.

She appreciates all that Michael does for her and their family, though there are times when she wishes he could be around a little more. They both assumed that as the girls got older, things would become easier, but the opposite is proving true, and Hannah sometimes feels as though she is parenting them alone.

When she thinks of those early days with Olivia as a newborn, much of what she can recall of the time is characterised by sleeplessness and fear. The days merged into one, a phase that seemed to her to be never-ending, and though she knew that the feelings she was experiencing were normal to most new mothers, she worried that there was something more, something she couldn't confess to anyone. Sometimes she couldn't bring herself to hold her own child. When Olivia cried – that piercing, shrill squawk that only tiny babies make – Hannah would find herself unable to go to her, wanting only to shut herself away from the sound somehow, to escape from her responsibilities and everything her life had suddenly become. She felt the isolation so intensely at times, it seemed it would break her. She reminds herself that it didn't, and that if she could get through those seemingly endless weeks, she can get through anything.

She has seen the way in which when certain things become easier, others become more challenging. As the relentlessness of Olivia's colic subsided, it gave way to teething and illness, and there were days when Hannah would forget to eat. She loved her daughter – she tried her very best to love her – but she knew she didn't love her in the right way, as she suspected other mothers loved their babies, and the knowledge of her emotional deficiencies hung over her like the darkest of clouds, exhausting her with the guilt it rained over her in frequent relentless downpours.

'Perhaps you'll tell your father how your day was,' she says, snapping herself back to the present. Her words are spoken with the tone of a threat. It is intended. 'Perhaps you'll tell him why you did what you did.'

There is a reaction from Olivia, though it is not what Hannah expected. There's a flicker behind her eyes, but it doesn't seem to be one of recognition. Instead, Olivia seems not to know what she is referring to. Could she have got this wrong? Has Michael got it wrong? Are they holding Olivia responsible for what happened here on Saturday night when really their daughter is blameless of any fault on this occasion?

'I won't be made to feel this way in my own home,' she says, knowing that Michael's intuition often proves itself correct, as annoying at times as that might be. 'Whatever you're trying to do, you won't intimidate me.'

She is lying, of course; she is already intimidated. Not by Olivia, but by her silence, and what she fears she might know. What she fears might come next.

'Come down and have your dinner,' she says, making it clear that this is an instruction and not a request.

Without objection, Olivia slides from the bed and makes her way to the door. Hannah follows her downstairs and they go into the kitchen. She serves their food in silence, inwardly shaken at the muted defiance her older daughter is so easily capable of. She knows what happened on Saturday, but she didn't so much as flinch when Hannah referred to it. Is she innocent, or is there something else behind her strange behaviour? As the three of them eat in silence, Hannah looks at Rosie, her head bowed over her dinner as though in prayer. She watches as her younger daughter spears a piece of broccoli with her fork and pops it into her mouth, chewing with her head still lowered, not wanting to be drawn into the strange situation playing out between her sister and her mother.

'Thanks for the food, Mum.'

Hannah gives Rosie a smile, watching as Olivia barely touches her meal. She has done this a lot recently, pushing her food from one side of the plate to the other, and in the past year her figure has changed dramatically, the youthful puppy fat she carried around her thighs and stomach now gone, replaced by slim legs and a tiny waistline.

After dinner is finished – Olivia's food left to go cold – both girls go upstairs to their bedrooms. Hannah also goes upstairs, tempted by the appeal of an early night. She wants nothing more than to change into a nightdress and climb beneath the duvet, for her brain to find sleep quickly and her mind to switch off until morning, but she doesn't allow herself to succumb. She needs to speak to Michael when he gets home.

She doesn't have to wait long. At just gone 8.30, she hears her husband's key in the front door. She listens to him move around downstairs; then, after a few minutes, he makes his way up to the bedroom. When he enters the room, his work shirt pulled untidily from his trousers and his tie loosened from its grip around his neck, he looks tired, his lethargy worn in the deep grooves at the corners of his glassy eyes.

He runs a hand over his balding scalp. He looks older than his forty-two years, age and the stress of work catching up with him, and she wishes she could slow time for them all. When they were younger, the age gap seemed much greater, and Hannah considers with some sadness the possibility that rather than her keeping him young, he has aged them both. She feels guilty for the thought that Michael might be anything but good for her. He is everything to her. He stayed by her side at a time when there was no one else to support her.

She remembers him as he was when they first met, so handsome and attentive; kinder to her than anyone else in her life had ever been. She feels sure that even had she not been physically attracted to him, she would have been drawn to him anyway, simply for the person he was. Those first, early days before the unimaginable happened were the happiest and most exciting of her life. She wishes she had known at the time just how quickly they would pass, and how vulnerable the two of them would be to things they had no control over.

'Everything okay?'

She gets up from the bed where she has been lying. 'Fine. Your dinner's in the fridge.'

'I don't really fancy it,' he says, pulling off his jacket. 'Will it keep until tomorrow?'

Hannah nods and takes the jacket from him, putting it over the back of a chair. 'My keys went missing today.'

'What do you mean?'

'I mean, I couldn't find them. But the girls were at school, and there was no one else here. I must have had them to get back into the house.'

'You've found them now, though?'

Hannah has gone through it all in her mind, countless times. She walked the girls to school and then came home. She locked the front door behind her once she was back inside the house and then set about her chores for that morning. The keys were left in the lock. When she went to leave just before lunchtime, they were nowhere to be found. By the time she was due to meet the girls from school, they were in the box where they're usually kept, the one that Michael bought so that this sort of thing would never happen. But it's impossible, she knows it is. They weren't there when she looked for them earlier. No one else was in the house.

'Yes,' she replies quietly. 'I've got them now.'

She feels Michael move nearer to her before his hand rests on her shoulders.

'Are you okay, love? You seem tense.'

She exhales beneath the weight of his hands, as though he is pressing all the tension and anxiety from her body. 'What are we going to do about Olivia?'

Behind her, Michael sighs. 'Is this about the weekend?' His hands slide from her, leaving her cold.

'I still think we should tell the police.'

There is a moment of silence before he speaks again. 'We've talked about this. I'll call them if you want me to, but we really need to consider it carefully. Is that what you really want, the police here? This doesn't just affect Olivia, does it?'

'I know that, but …' Hannah's sentence trails off into silence. She knows what she wants to say. What if it wasn't Olivia? What if a stranger was responsible and that stranger is still free to do the same to someone else, or even to return to their home if he chooses?

And yet she knows that whoever it was, the person was no stranger to her. Whoever it was, he or she knows something about her, something she doesn't want made public.

She already knows how Michael will respond to her suggestion that they contact the police. She knows what his counter-argument will be. He's right, of course. If there is any chance that Olivia was involved, the police will find it. She will be marked by it for life, and so will they.

'I'm sorry,' she says quietly. 'I just can't stand the thought of it. I want to feel safe here.'

She feels his hands return to her, rubbing warmth into her shoulders and beginning to ease some of the tensions of the day from her body. 'You *are* safe here,' he tries to reassure her. 'But ...' It's his turn to fade to silence.

'But what?'

'Liar,' he says, a word that stings Hannah's ears as though she has been slapped. For a moment, she thinks he is accusing rather than repeating. 'It's just ... I've been thinking about it all day. If it was Olivia who wrote that, what does it mean? Who's the liar?'

Hannah swallows. The noise is so loud in her ears that she's sure it must be audible to him. 'I don't know,' she lies, recognising the irony.

Michael sighs again. He sits on the edge of the bed and pulls her down to sit beside him, and she rests her head on his shoulder as his arm snakes around her to hold her close. It feels good to have him home, to have him here beside her, a temporary presence before he is gone again. She knew that he would be able to reassure her; she trusts him to know what to do for the best.

'You need a break, love.'

'From what?'

'Olivia's behaviour ... I know it's been difficult for you.'

'It's not difficult,' she says, lying again. 'I just want to know what I'm supposed to do about it.'

'You and me both. But we knew this would happen one day, didn't we? We talked about it.'

Hannah gives a slight nod, not really wanting to acknowledge the conversation that happened so long ago now she hoped Michael might have forgotten all about it. Yes, they knew that these days would arrive, but that doesn't mean she is any more prepared for them.

'We need to consider what we spoke about. Olivia's behaviour is a problem. This is only the start. She's going to push us until she thinks we'll break. And it's not just about us any more, is it? We have to think about what's best for Rosie too.'

With her head still on her husband's shoulder, Hannah starts to cry silent tears. She isn't sure whether they are tears of sadness or of anger, only that they are raw and painful, that they have been held back for far too long, and that many of them are for herself. She has tried her best, but she has failed.

'I'll look into it tomorrow,' he says.

EIGHT

OLIVIA

On Tuesday morning, Olivia decides that the only way she is going to get through the day is to shut her mind off as though pretending she no longer exists, and that her life isn't the continual humiliation it has become. She knows it isn't likely to be easy to ignore the rumours that follow her around the school grounds like a stray dog, a suspicion confirmed when she passes a group of sixth-form boys in the corridor and one of them wolf-whistles at her, sending his friends into bursts of spiteful laughter. She feels herself colour instantly, her cheeks warming in a swell of embarrassment so intense it makes her feel sick. Was what she did on Friday night really all that bad, or was it just because it was her, the girl no one expected it of?

She grips the handle of the bag on her shoulder and wonders whether Miss Johnson would allow her to work from her classroom for the day. Despite what happened there just yesterday, that classroom feels like a safe place in comparison to the rest of the school grounds, but she doesn't like to ask. The answer is likely to be no, and anyway, she has spent too much of her life hiding away in the shadows.

During her IT lesson, when she is supposed to be working on a spreadsheet, she accesses the internet and tentatively types what she is looking for into the search engine. She has chosen the computer in the furthest corner of the room, keeping one eye on Mr Matthews and the other on the screen. She is in luck; Mr Matthews is engrossed in a discussion with a table of geeky boys at the front of the room about the denouement of some Marvel comic series of films, and doesn't seem too interested in what the rest of the class is up to. Beside her, Ollie Morris is playing a game on a website he shouldn't be on. He glances at her when he feels her staring at him, before returning his attention to the game. He too is uninterested in what she is doing, and Olivia supposes that on this occasion, she should feel grateful that nobody cares enough to pay her any notice.

She scans the list of search results that appear on the screen when she presses Enter. There are more than she thought. Taking out her planner, she quickly copies down the names and numbers before closing the internet and returning the book to her bag. She opens the spreadsheet she's supposed to be working on, but her mind is elsewhere. It is always elsewhere, even more so recently. Her mother has been lying to her. Olivia wants to know why.

The rest of the morning passes without event, which Olivia is grateful for. Her brain switches off during history, her thoughts trapped in the details of what she needs to find and do, and during biology, she does the bare minimum she can get away with without her idleness being spotted by the teacher. By the time lunch arrives, her mind is set on a plan. She needs somewhere quiet, somewhere no staff or other students will overhear her.

'Miss?'

Miss Johnson looks up from the screen of her computer.

'Olivia. Everything okay?'

Olivia nods. 'I, uh … I wanted to say sorry, that's all.'

'Sorry? What for?'

Olivia steps into the classroom and closes the door behind her. 'The way I spoke to you yesterday. I shouldn't have snapped at you like that.'

'It's fine, you don't need to apologise for that.'

'I was wondering, uh ... would it be okay for me to sit in here for lunch? I don't mean to eat – I've already had something,' she lies. 'I just mean to sit in here, to, uh, get some work done.' She realises she is rambling now, that her words are punctuated with too many pauses and stutters, so she stops talking, hoping she hasn't made herself appear too suspicious.

Miss Johnson gives her a sympathetic smile. The awkwardness of the incident during yesterday's lesson is standing between them, an invisible cause of discomfort for them both and something that neither of them wants to outwardly acknowledge. 'You don't fancy the library?'

The words feel like a personal rejection. Their effect must be evident on Olivia's face, as Miss Johnson's expression changes instantly and she ushers her to a desk with a wave of her hand. 'You can sit in here, but I haven't had lunch yet. Will you be okay on your own for a while?'

With a nod, Olivia thanks her. She pulls books from her rucksack, making it look as though she is about to focus on some work. Miss Johnson takes her handbag from beneath her desk, leaving the classroom door open behind her as she heads for the canteen.

As soon as she is gone, Olivia closes the door, then scrabbles in her bag for her notebook, retrieving the list of numbers she noted down during the IT lesson. She unlocks her mobile and taps in the first number, knowing she has a limited amount of time before the teacher returns.

The phone rings just three times before it is answered.

'Could I speak to Eleanor Medway, please?' She can hear her voice shaking as she speaks.

'I'm sorry,' the woman says, a slight note of bemusement in her tone, 'there's no one here of that name.'

'Okay,' Olivia says, her nervousness replaced with disappoint-ment. 'Sorry.' She ends the call and quickly taps in the next number. It rings for what feels like forever, and Olivia is about to hang up when someone finally answers.

'Could I speak to Eleanor Medway, please?'

'Who?' the man asks.

'Eleanor Medway,' Olivia repeats, trying to keep her voice steady. Her palm is sweating, her grip loose on the phone. She glances at the classroom door, wondering how much time she has before Miss Johnson returns with her lunch.

'Just a minute, please,' the man says. He sounds as clueless as she is, Olivia thinks. She waits, scanning the list of phone numbers that remains, knowing she doesn't have enough time now to try them all. A few moments later, the man returns. 'I'm sorry,' he says. 'There's no one here called Eleanor Medway.'

'Okay. Sorry.'

On the third call, much the same happens, except the woman who answers asks Olivia who she is. She hangs up, not wanting to explain the purpose of her call. She glances at the clock; taps a fourth number into her phone. A female voice answers.

'Could I speak to Eleanor Medway, please?'

'I don't think she's finished her lunch yet,' the woman says, and Olivia feels a jumble of emotions knot in her stomach, making her feel sick with anticipation. There is a flutter in her chest like the wings of a tiny bird, and she tells herself not to get carried away by hoping for too much too soon.

'Would you mind calling back a bit later?' the woman asks.

'No, that's fine,' she says hurriedly.

'Can I ask who's calling?'

Olivia hesitates. 'It's her daughter,' she lies.

'Okay, well I'll let her know you called and that you'll speak to her later, all right?'

'Great. Thank you.'

When she looks up, Miss Johnson is in the doorway, a baguette wrapped in cellophane in her hand and a raised eyebrow questioning the phone that Olivia is holding. 'Why was the door closed?'

'Sorry. My mum called.' It's amazing how easily the lies fall, she thinks. Now that telling these little white lies has become a default setting, she doesn't know that she'll be able to stop. There is something addictive about the deception of it all.

Miss Johnson eyes her sceptically, obviously not quite believing her. Olivia vows to become better, more convincing. She smiles at the teacher and puts her phone and notebook back into her bag.

'You know, Olivia, if you want to talk to me about anything, you can.'

Olivia glances down at the books on the desk. She wonders what it would feel like to talk to someone about what is going on. Most girls her age would be able to confide in their mothers, but Olivia's mother is the very person she can't speak to. It would be lovely to be able to talk to Miss Johnson, like having an auntie or an older sister. Olivia has never really had a friend, not a close one that she can share her secrets with. Everything she wants to say gathers on her tongue, the effort of holding it all in almost choking her.

'I'm fine, miss,' she says, not quite enjoying this lie as much as the last. 'Honestly. Thanks, though.'

Miss Johnson nods and takes her lunch to her desk, where she returns her attention to the screen of her computer. Olivia feels her stomach roil. She knows where Eleanor is, where exactly she can find her. Only she realises she doesn't actually know. She has an address, but it doesn't mean anything to her.

'Miss?'

Miss Johnson lifts her head. She has a crumb of bread at the side of her mouth and wipes it self-consciously with the back of a hand.

'Sorry,' Olivia says, feeling embarrassment rise to her face in a flush that is becoming a second skin. 'Could I ask you a favour?'

Miss Johnson nods, her mouth still full of a bite of sandwich.

'Could you tell me how I get to Templeton Road?'

'Is that in town? I'm not sure I know it. Have you got maps on your phone?'

Olivia shakes her head. She waits as Miss Johnson closes the file she has been working on and opens the internet browser. 'I'll look it up for you now,' she says. She taps the street name into the search engine and waits for the results. 'According to this, it's not too far from the south beach. About five roads back from the promenade.'

She smiles at Olivia as if this is enough, as though Olivia should now know how to get there. Olivia returns the smile with a blank expression that gives away her ignorance.

'Shall I write down directions for you?' Miss Johnson suggests.

'Thanks.'

While she jots down the directions, Olivia finds herself staring at the top of the teacher's head, and at the dark glossy hair that falls over her shoulders. She is wearing a fitted top with a Peter Pan collar that manages to make her look even younger. Olivia understands why she is so popular, why the boys fancy her and the girls want to be like her.

'What's on Templeton Road anyway?' Miss Johnson asks, still writing.

'Oh, just a shop,' Olivia tells her, feeling guilty for this lie, though unsure why. 'I've seen a dress online.' It sounds such a normal thing to say, something any of the other girls in her class might say. And yet from Olivia's mouth and with her voice, the words sound alien.

She stands when Miss Johnson holds out the sheet of paper, goes to the desk and thanks her again. Her fingers shake as the list of directions passes from the teacher's hand to hers, and she wonders whether Miss Johnson notices the trembling as she tries to still it.

'I'd better go,' she says, hurriedly packing her books into her bag. She senses Miss Johnson's eyes on her, questioning the sudden rush to leave, and it makes her want to get from the room all the sooner. 'Thanks again, miss.'

She clatters clumsily from the room, the door banging shut behind her, and narrowly avoids someone in the corridor, whether a student or a teacher she doesn't know. Her mind is elsewhere, and she knows it won't be at rest until she finds out the truth. She needs to go to Templeton Road today, and she will willingly face the consequences.

Dear Diary,

I need to find a way to make her pay for what she is doing to me. Every day, it feels as though these walls are closing in around me tighter and tighter, like eventually they will squeeze the breath from my lungs and I will die here. Maybe that is what she is hoping for. I've seen the way she looks at me, like she knows what I'm thinking, and I'm sure she's planning something. I can't trust her. I need to get away from here, but the longer I leave it, the harder it is to do. It should be easy, but it just isn't, and I don't have anyone to try to explain it to. It doesn't even make sense to me. I wish I was somewhere else, just anywhere. I don't want to be me any more.

NINE

HANNAH

Hannah is out in the back garden tending to the flower beds when she hears the telephone. The house phone rarely rings these days; when it does, it is usually telesales or automated messages, and she invariably puts the receiver down without listening to what the person at the other end of the line has to say. Today is different.

'Mrs Walters? This is Sally Baker, one of the receptionists from St Andrew's Primary School.'

Hannah feels a stirring in the pit of her stomach telling her that something is wrong. The school never calls her. Something has happened.

'Is Rosie okay?' she asks, hearing the wobble in the words.

'There's been an accident,' Sally starts to say, but Hannah barely understands what comes next. *Climbing frame … fall … ambulance* … Each word blurs into the next to form a white noise in her head.

'I'm coming,' she says. 'I'll get a taxi straight there.'

She puts the phone down and runs to the kitchen, hoping there is enough change in the emergency fund tin. It should only cost a few pounds, but she hasn't looked in the tin in so long; she has no idea how much or how little is in there. Shaking the coins into her hand, she goes back to the phone and calls for a taxi. Then she searches for her mobile and calls Michael, but it goes straight to answerphone. She leaves a message, hoping it isn't too long until he picks it up.

The taxi arrives a short while later, though those minutes feel like an age to Hannah, and she suspects she might have got there quicker if she ran. She wonders whether the ambulance is already there, or whether the receptionist said that one had been called. She should have listened more carefully, but it was so hard to take everything in. She just wants to get to her daughter.

When the driver pulls up at the school gates, she looks up and down the street for signs of an ambulance. There isn't one. Either it hasn't arrived yet or Rosie has already been taken to hospital. She empties the handful of coins into the driver's palm, not knowing whether she is giving him enough or too much. 'Keep the change,' she tells him, hoping that the latter will be the case, and that if it isn't, he won't bother to stop and count through it all now.

She gets out of the car and runs to the front door, where she presses the buzzer. 'Rosie Walters' mum,' she says, and the door bleeps as it is opened for her to go in. There is a woman at reception, but whether it is Sally or another of the staff members, she doesn't know; she can't remember all their names.

'Where's Rosie?' she asks breathlessly.

'Mrs Walters,' the woman says. 'Is everything okay?'

'Is she still here? Please take me to her.'

The woman gets up from her chair and emerges from a door to the side. 'Is everything okay?' she asks again.

'Has she gone already?'

'Gone where?' the woman asks, studying her with a raised eyebrow and a look of concern that Hannah resents.

'I got a call,' Hannah explains, feeling frustration build in her chest. 'From Sally. She said Rosie had been in an accident.' She sees the receptionist glance at someone just behind her, and turns to see a male member of staff at the door of one of the offices.

'Everything all right?' he asks.

'Will everyone stop asking that!' Hannah takes a deep breath and exhales loudly, trying to calm the anger she feels bubbling in her chest. 'I had a call from Sally,' she says again, trying to stay calm. 'She said my daughter, Rosie, had been in an accident.'

'Rosie Walters?' the man says. 'I've just seen her in the hall.'

Hannah sets off down the corridor, dreading what she'll find when she gets to the hall. When the woman on the phone told her Rosie had fallen from the climbing frame, she must have meant the ones in the hall used for PE lessons, not the ones outside in the playground as Hannah assumed. She wonders who is with Rosie; whether the school has a competent first-aider.

The receptionist runs to keep up with her. 'Mrs Walters,' she says, 'there must have been a mistake …'

But Hannah isn't listening. When she gets to the hall, she yanks open the double doors. Inside, a class of children wearing gym shorts and T-shirts are running in and out of coloured cones, the sound of their laughter echoing from the walls. She looks around frantically for Rosie, bewildered when she sees her daughter run past in a sweaty, giggling blur of red hair and bright white trainers.

'Rosie!' She flings out an arm, almost knocking the girl over as she passes.

Rosie makes a sudden stop, her trainers squeaking on the parquet floor. 'Mum. What are you doing here?'

Hannah turns to the receptionist. 'What's going on?' she asks, her tone accusing.

'That's what I was trying to tell you in the corridor. Sally couldn't have called you – she doesn't work on Tuesdays.'

Hannah looks at her incredulously, the woman's words not quite registering in her brain. 'Sally called me,' she repeats slowly. 'She said Rosie had been involved in an accident.'

The receptionist glances awkwardly at the nearest children. The room has fallen into silence now, the panting of breathless young lungs the only sound. 'Let's go back to reception,' she suggests. 'Rosie's fine, and that's the main thing.' She gives Rosie a smile, which only manages to make Hannah more frustrated. She wants to say so, but she doesn't.

She tells Rosie quietly that she'll see her later before leaving the class to resume their exercise. She follows the receptionist back down the corridor, feeling foolish and embarrassed, but most of all angry. Why would someone want to do this to her? She had thought the worst, imagining Rosie in countless awful predicaments. If it was meant as a practical joke, then it really wasn't funny.

'Would you like a cup of tea, Mrs Walters?'

'No. Thank you. I just want to know what's going on.'

'Okay. Look,' the woman says, gesturing to a chair. 'Why don't you wait here for a moment and I'll go and see if I can get hold of Sally. I've been the only person on reception this morning, so I know no one else would have called you.'

Hannah pats her jacket, locating her mobile phone. 'I'll just call my husband.'

The woman nods before heading back behind reception. Hannah feels her eyes on her as she leaves the main doors and goes to call her husband from just inside the school gates. Michael answers after just a few rings.

'Is Rosie okay?'

He knows she would never normally contact him while he's at work, so the call alone is enough to signal that all is not right. Hannah begins to tell him everything that has happened that morning, her words falling from her in a hurried, jumbled mess.

'Hannah, slow down. Is Rosie okay?'

'She's fine.'

Her husband's sigh of relief is audible. 'Look,' he tells her. 'Take a deep breath and try to calm down. You've obviously had a shock, but Rosie's all right, that's all that matters. We'll talk about it when I get home, okay?'

Hannah wants to talk about it now, though she knows there's little more that can be said or done over the phone. He's going to start thinking she's unstable, she thinks, what with losing the keys and now this. Reluctantly she tells him she'll see him later, before ending the call.

When she goes back into the school, the receptionist is waiting for her at the front desk. 'I've just spoken to Sally and she doesn't know anything about a call to you, Mrs Walters. She's been at her son's swimming gala all day.'

'It's okay,' Hannah says, raising a hand. It's really not okay, but it's clear that the school doesn't know anything about the phone call, and the main thing is that Rosie is still here, and she is safe. Hannah doesn't want to lose her composure in front of this woman, which has already been so close to happening. She will be the talk of the staffroom, no doubt, the crazy lady who came racing into the school talking nonsense about a phone call that none of them knows anything about.

The receptionist is looking at her with that very expression of pity that Hannah doesn't want to attract.

'Can I call you a taxi?'

'No,' Hannah replies. 'Thank you. I can walk home.'

She leaves the building and heads out of the school gates, grateful for the cool air that she swallows down in greedy gulps. An awful, very real possibility has taken root in her brain, and she knows that it is justified this time, supported by everything else that has taken place over the last few days. If no one from the school made that call, then someone else did, someone who wanted to scare her. It would be easy for anyone to find the name of a receptionist at the school – all they would need to do is search online for the website and find a list of staff names. Who would be malicious enough to fake a call like that? Who would know exactly what it would take to unnerve her in such a way?

Hannah shoves her hands into the pockets of her jacket as she crosses the road, her fingers curling to make fists. She doesn't want to think there's even the smallest chance it could be true, but she is sick of pushing aside what is staring her in the face just to replace it with something that she can only hope might hurt less. She needs to feel this pain. She deserves to.

There is only one possible answer to the question of who might have been behind this.

Olivia.

TEN

OLIVIA

Olivia stands at the end of the pier and looks out across the water, breathing in a wave of cool fresh air. It is a clear day, though chilly, and she pulls her coat around her chest, folding her arms to keep herself warm against the breeze that comes in from the wide expanse of grey sea. She has found Templeton Road and the address to which she is headed, but she wanted to come here first, to just stand at this spot and take in the view: the seagulls flying overhead, the railings that run the length of the pier; the water that stretches beyond it until it tips over the earth's edge, out of sight. It is grey-blue, like no other colour she has seen. If she were asked to describe it to someone, she wouldn't be able to compare it to anything else. She wouldn't have the words to tell them how it makes her feel.

Other than the noise of the gulls and the waves that lick the pebble beach beneath her, Olivia doesn't hear a sound. She is used to silence, although this is a kind of silence that she believes she could happily live with. Tipping her head back, she inhales the air as though breathing the stillness in, swallowing it down, storing it in her lungs so she can keep it, re-energise herself with it later.

She wishes she had some money with her. There is a café selling fish and chips at the entrance to the pier, and the smell of vinegar made her stomach rumble as she stepped onto the wooden boards that led her to where she now stands. Opposite it, there is a tiny sweet shop, an old-fashioned place selling pear drops and humbugs and an array of other flavours from a collection of glass jars that line the shelves behind the small strip of counter. Olivia wanted to go inside, just to look, but the owner was looking at her oddly – or maybe he was simply returning her own expression, she can't be sure.

Pushing away thoughts of her hunger, she turns her back to the promenade and everything she can't have and stares out over the great expanse of ocean that looms in front of her. She imagines what it would be like to jump into its icy depths, to feel its cold grip tighten its fingers on her skin and pull her below its dull surface. As a child, she believed in mermaids. She wanted to be one, which made bath time easier for her parents, never having to face the fight of getting her upstairs and into the tub. She loved the feel of water on her skin and on her face, and sometimes, older now, she submerges herself in the shallows of the bath, wondering how it might feel to stay beneath the surface. Perhaps she will do it one day, she thinks.

It took her over half an hour to walk here from school, and pulling herself from the dark turn of her thoughts, Olivia realises that there is little over an hour left before school finishes and she will be late home if she doesn't move quickly and do what she is here for. There will be more questions to answer, more anger to face. She has her own questions, ones she recited over and over in her head while walking to this place, and yet now she is here, they all seem to have left her, blown away on the wind and stolen from her by the sea. The thought makes her turn and head back to the promenade. If she delays her purpose any longer, she knows she will talk herself out of it completely.

A couple of minutes later, back at Templeton Road, Olivia tentatively presses the bell of Sea Breeze House. There is an intercom at the door, with a keypad underneath. She wonders who knows the code; whether it is just the staff, or if regular visitors can use it to gain entry. She waits a while before pressing the bell again. A few moments later, a young woman comes to open the door. She is pale, and her hair is lank, scraped back from her face in a knot that looks too tight, pulling painfully at her temples. She doesn't appear to be much older than Olivia herself. The girl raises an eyebrow expectantly.

'I'm here to see Eleanor,' Olivia explains, her heart pumping with the words. 'I'm her granddaughter.'

The girl ushers her into the building, looking up and down the corridor as though searching for another member of staff. She doesn't look as though she belongs here, and Olivia appreciates the irony of the thought. She waits for the girl to question her or make a comment about the fact that she has never been here before, but when she says nothing, Olivia wonders whether she is new here. When the girl can't find another member of staff to hand, she points to her left.

'She's in her room,' she says, obviously expecting Olivia to know where this is.

'Thanks.'

Olivia follows the corridor, glancing at each closed door in turn. Beside each one is a small plaque with the name of the resident. The nursing home has recently been repainted, and the smell of gloss lingers. It is an unpleasant reminder of home, and of the smell that has haunted the kitchen since Saturday night. Whatever happened there, Olivia's mother believes her guilty of it. She no longer cares. Her mother can think what she likes.

Olivia has never been in one of these places before and had no idea what to expect before arriving. The sounds scare her. Somewhere along the hallway, from a room in which the door has been left ajar, an elderly lady is howling, her wails interspersed with the repetition of the word 'mama', a pitiful pair of syllables that makes Olivia at once sad and repulsed in a way she can't justify and feels ashamed by. A woman wearing a blue tabard walks past the room, oblivious to the patient's pleas, her face impassive. Stepping to one side as the woman passes, Olivia takes a deep breath. She wants to go home, and yet she never wants to see this place again. She doesn't want to be here, but there are too many things she needs to know.

She passes another five names before she reaches the plaque that reads *Eleanor Medway*. She doesn't know what she should do, whether to knock or just push the door open, so she pauses for a moment, waiting for her heart to stop racing, then knocks gently. When there is no reply, she knocks again, this time giving the door a push to see whether it will yield.

'Eleanor,' she says softly, not sure of the welcome she might receive.

The room isn't what she's expecting, though what she was expecting she isn't quite sure. The entrance to the building and its corridors were clinical and sparse, yet here there is colour: paintings on the walls, patterned throws across the bed, pot plants on the windowsill. She realises now that she imagined the room would resemble a hospital ward, yet someone has made efforts to create a comfortable place, something that might look vaguely like home. She wonders if that person is her mother.

Eleanor is sitting in a chair in the corner, hunched forward. The top of her back is arched painfully, and she is staring at the television that sits on top of the cheap chest of drawers against the opposite wall, its wood veneer peeling and curling at the corners, watching people search for something that might be of value among tables of junk at a car boot sale. The sound is turned off.

'Have you brought a cup of tea?' she asks. 'I've been waiting ages for a cup of tea.'

She doesn't turn her head; she hasn't realised yet that Olivia isn't staff. Perhaps she wouldn't realise even if she was to look. Olivia has never seen advanced old age like this, not up close and in real life. Her only experience of the elderly has come from television, and that has been limited: the grandmothers in gravy advertisements who cook dinner for the family on a Sunday; the old men in soap operas who sit in the corners of pubs passing judgement on the world as it goes on around them.

She wonders how many people Eleanor sees in a day, and how many of those people talk to her, really talk to her, not just to ask her if she would like a cup of tea. She feels a pang of something like pain in her chest, but she can't put a name to what it is.

'I can find someone to get you a cup if you like,' she says, and when she speaks, she doesn't recognise the sound of her own voice. She sounds strained, high-pitched, as though her voice is coming from someone else.

Eleanor looks over for the first time. 'Who are you?' she snaps.

'Olivia.'

She isn't sure what is wrong with this woman, whether she is unwell in some way or just elderly, but she thinks she sees a flash of recognition behind Eleanor's eyes when she says her name.

'Who?

'Olivia,' she says again, and a new possibility occurs to her; the possibility that this woman might have never heard of her before and has no idea that she exists.

'Well make yourself useful and open the window a bit – I'm sweating cobs in here.'

Eleanor watches her as Olivia goes to the window and leans over to raise the latch.

'Waif of a thing, aren't you?'

Olivia has no experience of elderly people; she doesn't know whether it's normal for them to just come out with whatever thoughts flit through their minds. The urge to respond with something sarcastic usually comes naturally to her, but she swallows down a potential reply and instead says nothing, smiling at Eleanor as she stands back and moves from blocking her view of the silent television.

'Where's your uniform?'

Olivia feels panic kick in. Clearly Eleanor thinks she's a member of staff.

'I don't work here,' she says, knowing instantly that she has said the wrong thing.

Eleanor grips the arms of her chair and tries to push herself upright. 'Who are you, then?' she asks again, her voice filled with panic. 'What are you doing in my room?'

She begins to try to push herself out of her chair, and Olivia notices the alarm cord that hangs just to the side of it. If Eleanor pulls it, someone will come to help her, then Olivia will be thrown out and she will never learn the truth. She'll never know what's going on. If the only person she can rely on to provide the truth is her mother, she knows that it will never see the light of day. Her mother is a liar. She lies about everything.

'Eleanor,' she says, trying her best to sound calm and in control, 'my name is Olivia. I'm family.'

'You're not my family,' Eleanor says, outraged at the suggestion. 'I don't know you. If it's money you're after, I haven't got any.'

'I don't want your money. I just … I need to ask you a few questions, that's all. About my mum.'

Eleanor narrows her eyes. She doesn't know who I'm talking about, Olivia thinks.

'Hannah. My mum is Hannah.'

Eleanor smiles now, and for the briefest of moments Olivia misreads the expression, welcoming it as a gesture of acknowledgement, maybe even of acceptance. She is wrong; she knows this as soon as the smile dips at each corner and turns into a grimace as quickly as it appeared.

'I don't know what you're talking about,' Eleanor says, shaking her head and retuning her attention to the television, where a woman is trying to persuade a seller to knock five pounds off the asking price for a small silver tortoise brooch. 'My Hannah doesn't have any children.'

ELEVEN

HANNAH

Hannah watches Rosie complete her homework at the kitchen table. A couple of times Rosie asks a question, but Hannah can offer little more than a 'hmm' or an 'I'm not sure' in response. Rosie might be doing maths, or she might be doing art, Hannah wouldn't know. Her mind is trapped in the day's events, and by the thought of Olivia, upstairs in her room, submerged in the silence she has chosen to keep herself in.

She doesn't want to think it possible, but the more her mind worries at the idea that Olivia might have been involved with that phone call in some way, the more it makes perfect sense. She obviously didn't physically make the call herself; she couldn't have, Hannah would have recognised her own daughter's voice. There is a chance she might have got one of her classmates to do it, though. Did the voice sound young? Hannah can't remember. In her panic over Rosie and what might have happened, she didn't pay attention to the voice, only to the words, and even those were blurred by her state of panic.

But is Olivia that close to anyone at school? She never mentions any friends, and Hannah finds it hard to believe that anyone would have done that for her, not when they would have known they would get into trouble if they were found out. Either way, Olivia's possible involvement preys on her consciousness, interrupting any other thoughts that might attempt to quash it.

'Mum?'

'Yes.'

'Can I ask you something?'

'Go on.'

'What was today all about? You know, at school?'

Hannah knew the question was coming. She is surprised it has taken this long to emerge. She smiles as though it was all a silly mistake, something she wishes was the case. 'Just a mix-up, that's all. Nothing to worry about.'

Rosie looks at her as though she wants to say something else, but instead she returns her focus to her exercise book. Hannah feels relief wash over her. She expected more of an inquisition, and is grateful that it hasn't come.

Ten minutes later, she goes up to Olivia's room.

'Your phone,' she says, extending an arm and holding out her hand.

She sees the panic on her daughter's face, though Olivia still refuses to react with words. Her expression is crestfallen, and Hannah wonders exactly what she will find when she checks through her call history. Will there be evidence of a phone call made to the house phone earlier today? If she finds it, she hasn't planned how she is going to react or what she is going to do about it.

Olivia hands over the phone grudgingly, slapping it into her mother's palm. Hannah eyes her with annoyance before unlocking it, going to the call history and scrolling through the results. She is met with immediate disappointment: the last call made from the phone was the week before, to Hannah's own mobile. She remembers the call now, about a forgotten schoolbook.

As she hands the phone back, Hannah doesn't miss the look that crosses Olivia's face before she is able to quickly erase it. For the briefest of moments, she appeared relieved. Hannah's mind begins to churn, wondering just what her daughter might be relieved about, what she feared her mother might see. At the same time, disappointment at finding nothing incriminating washes over her, and it surprises her that she should feel this way. Would knowing Olivia was responsible for the call make it easier to manage in some way, or is it better that the person who phoned her remains anonymous, lending bliss to her ignorance? She isn't sure; all she knows is that the strangeness of the week that lies behind them can't be coincidental. Somehow, Saturday night is linked to this afternoon. All she needs to do is work out how and why.

'Why do you hate me so much?'

She hasn't thought about the question before asking it; her brain hasn't gifted her the time. Instead, the words fall from her mouth in a tone she realises is too panicked, ugly in their desperation and shameful in their exposure. She doesn't want to show Olivia any sign of weakness, though she fears she already has.

'Tell me.'

She hears the anger in her own voice, but it appears to have no effect on Olivia, who sits, unflinching, staring at her as though all of this is normal.

'Tell me!'

She feels the heat in her face, which is ablaze with frustration, and she knows she needs to stop. If Michael was here now, what would he tell her? Calm down. You're the parent. Stay in control.

She waits a moment, giving Olivia a chance to do the right thing and finally say something, but when there is still nothing, she turns her back on her daughter and leaves the room, slamming the door shut behind her. She stands on the landing, catching her breath and reprimanding herself for what just happened.

When she is calmer, she goes downstairs and returns to the kitchen, where Rosie's attention is still focused on her homework. A short while later, she is relieved to hear the sound of Michael's key in the lock of the front door. She listens to him take off his coat and shoes in the hallway, and moments later he appears at the kitchen door. 'How are my favourite ladies?' he asks.

Hannah gives him a smile, but Rosie barely acknowledges him, immersed in whatever it is she is doing. He looks at his wife with a silent question, one eyebrow raised. She nods. I'm fine, it says, though they both know this is a lie.

'Rosie, would you like to watch TV for a bit?'

Rosie looks up at her mother with surprise. She is barely midway through her homework, and television is rarely permitted on weekdays. Not waiting for a second offer, she gets up from the table and heads to the living room, leaving the door open behind her. Hannah follows and closes it, wanting to keep to themselves whatever words might now pass between her and Michael.

'Good day?' she asks him, as though everything is normal.

'Fine. Are you okay, love? What happened?'

Hannah smiles, but the gesture is forced, and within moments of its appearance she is crying, hot tears rolling down her cheeks as she tries to swallow the lump of embarrassment that is lodged in her throat. She hates what this past week has made her, emotional and unbalanced, and she doesn't want anyone to see her like this, least of all Michael.

'Come here.' He moves towards her, arms outstretched, and Hannah falls into his embrace. 'Tell me all about it.'

Hannah does so, properly this time, filling in the details that she missed during their harried phone call earlier in the day. She tells him what was said, and how she rushed to the school fearing the worst. She tells him about the reaction of the receptionist and about seeing Rosie in the hall, running around without a care in the world. She tells him about the receptionist's phone call to Sally and how she knew nothing of the incident, and about how embarrassed and foolish she herself felt about it all. She feels sure that the receptionist thought she was making it all up, that she is mentally unstable in some way.

'I don't understand it, Michael, why would someone do that to me? It's not funny, it's sick.' Hannah knows how she sounds. Even to her own ears, her voice is shrill and erratic.

Michael closes his grip around her, holding her close. She rests her head on his chest, can feel him breathing in the smell of her shampoo. 'It must all have been a mistake somehow.'

'But how?' She raises a hand to her face to wipe her tears dry. 'I don't think it was. I think someone wanted to hurt me, and they used Rosie to do it. I tried to get the number from the phone when I got back home, but it was withheld.'

Michael is quiet for a moment. 'But like you said, why would someone want to do that?' he says eventually. 'It doesn't make any sense, love.'

It seems to Hannah that much of what has been happening in the house recently doesn't make a lot of sense. She is still plagued by thoughts of Saturday night, and by the solitary word sprayed on the kitchen cupboards. The thought of a stranger being in their home has made her feel constantly sick, stealing her sleep and turning her into a zombie during the day. Someone wants to unsettle her. Someone wants to make her feel as though she is losing her mind, and they are managing to do exactly that.

She places her palms on Michael's chest and pushes herself away from him. When she looks up at him, she knows he is thinking exactly what she is. 'You don't think it's possible, do you?'

'What?'

She glances to the kitchen door, though she knows that both it and the living room door are shut. 'Olivia. You've thought it too, haven't you?'

Michael sighs and tilts his head to one side, studying her as though she is an object of pity. The look fills Hannah with frustration.

'Don't do that,' she says, turning away from him. 'Just say what you want to, Michael; you don't have to look at me like that.' She flicks the switch on the kettle and reaches to the cupboard above for a mug. 'Do you want one?'

'Go on then.'

As she is taking tea bags out of the ceramic pot that sits beside the kettle, Hannah feels her husband's hands rest on her waist. When he speaks, his breath hits the side of her neck. 'I wasn't looking at you in any way,' he tells her, the words soft in her ear. 'I worry about you, that's all.'

'I don't need your concern,' she says, shaking herself free of him. 'I need you to tell me the truth. You've said there's a chance she might be responsible for what happened here on Saturday. What about this? Do you think she might be involved?'

His silence answers her question. He doesn't want to think it, but that can't stop him from doing so, not if the thought has taken root and is already beginning to grow. They can't escape what Olivia is and who she might yet become.

Hannah makes their tea in silence before placing both mugs on the table. She takes a seat, waiting for Michael to join her.

'Why does she hate me so much?'

'She doesn't hate you, Hannah.'

'She does. I've seen the way she looks at me, and not just this past week. She's always been like it. And now this refusal to speak to me. She hates me.'

'She's refusing to speak to me as well,' Michael reminds her. 'Does she hate me too?'

Possibly, Hannah thinks, although she says nothing. Michael reaches across the table and takes her hand. 'Look, Olivia's fifteen going on twenty-five. This is a phase, we've got to remember that, okay. We've got through other things and we'll get through this.'

Other things. Hannah meets his eye, knowing that their minds have taken them to the same place. She doesn't want to return there, but she fears that soon she might have to, whether or not she is willing.

'It's not normal for her to stay this silent for so long,' she tells him. 'A day I could have understood. Two, maybe. But not this. She's trying to punish us.'

'Punish us? Punish us for what, Hannah?'

His voice is so soothing, his tone so calming, that she could almost allow herself to believe that he is right. Yet she can't. There are too many other contradictory factors; things she hasn't wanted to think about but can't stop herself from dwelling on.

'What if this is just in her, Michael?'

'What do you mean, "in her"?

Hannah looks at him long and hard, her eyes widening to communicate her meaning. 'You know what I'm saying,' she tells him, not wanting to have to spell it out. 'There are things we can't control. No matter what we try to do, we can't account for whatever nature is in her, can we?'

'Oh,' Michael says. 'The nature–nurture debate again?'

Hannah sighs tiredly. 'You can't just dismiss it. She's not like Rosie, is she? They couldn't be less alike.'

'And the same could be said for most siblings.' Michael stands and opens the door. 'I'm going for a shower. You need to stop this, Hannah, it isn't good for anyone. You're only torturing yourself with it.'

When he has gone, Hannah sits back and closes her eyes. The teas she made are left to go cold while she contemplates everything that hasn't been said. She has never wanted to articulate it, but she's beginning to feel that somebody needs to. She hates herself for feeling this way about her own child. She wants to believe the best of her daughter. She wants to believe that she is a good mother. Sometimes, though, she's far from sure of either.

TWELVE

OLIVIA

'Why haven't you told your mother about us? She doesn't even know that Rosie and I exist.'

Olivia looks at herself in the mirror of the girls' toilets, holding her own gaze as though her reflection might offer her an answer. There are so many things she wants to ask her mother, so many things she needs to know, but doing so would mean breaking her silence, something she is not prepared to do. Her mother has kept so much from her for so long that living in ignorance for a little longer will do her no harm.

She is broken from her thoughts by the sound of laughter as a group of girls from the year below clatter through the door. There are three of them; two ignore her, but the third throws her a look that Olivia catches in the mirror, the glance accompanied by a snigger the girl makes no attempt to stifle. She could be imagining it is directed at her – they were laughing when they entered the room, before they'd even seen her there – yet Olivia can't shake the feeling that she is the butt of every joke. She wonders for a second if they heard her talking to herself in the mirror, and her cheeks warm at the thought. Before she has time to turn any redder, she grabs her bag from the floor and leaves the toilets.

She hasn't even made it as far as her registration class when she hears her name being called down the corridor by the head of year. Mr Lewis is a PE teacher, built like a rugby prop forward, and to anyone who doesn't know him he might appear to be the kind of person not to be messed with. Most of the kids at school know differently, though; beneath the bullish exterior, he is as soft and malleable as a ball of plasticine. Plenty of the girls have got away with all sorts after turning on the waterworks in his office, and according to some, as soon as 'time of the month' is mentioned, he is quick to let misdemeanours slip. Olivia wonders whether she'll have the confidence to try to get away with either.

'Yes, sir,' she says, turning to his call.

'Can I have a word, please, Olivia?'

He gestures to an empty classroom and she follows him in. 'Mrs Peterson says you weren't in your biology lesson after lunch yesterday. You were in school, though, weren't you? You're marked in on the register.'

Olivia looks down at her hands and says nothing. She hears her stomach rumble; she can't remember the last time she ate something.

'You've got exams coming up. Don't let things slip now, not when you're this close.'

'Sorry, sir.'

He looks at her expectantly, waiting for more.

'Where were you, then? This isn't like you, is it.'

It's said as a statement rather than a question, so Olivia doesn't respond. There are a lot of things that aren't like her, but not necessarily through choice. Nobody really expects anything of her, so that's what she gives them. She wonders how it would feel to do something completely unlike her, something so unexpected that it would make people sit up and take notice.

I went to visit my grandmother, she says in her head. *Turns out she doesn't know I exist. Any idea why my mother would keep me a secret, Mr Lewis?*

'I had to go home,' she says.

Mr Lewis raises an eyebrow, still waiting for the rest of the explanation. Olivia looks him in the eye before glancing down. 'I started … you know …'

When she looks up, Mr Lewis's face has already started to flush an uncomfortable shade of pink. 'Right,' he says awkwardly. 'Okay. Next time, uh, try to see one of the female teachers first, okay? Right. Off you get to registration then.'

Olivia thanks him quietly before leaving the room, not quite believing that she's got away with it so easily. Now she sees why the other kids in her year take advantage of him. He makes it so easy for them; why wouldn't they treat him the way they do? Maybe that's where she's been going wrong, she thinks. She's treated the way she has allowed herself to be treated.

She gets to her registration class just as the bell sounds in the corridor, and the rest of the morning passes uneventfully, each lesson blending into the next until English arrives. The class files into the room in relative silence, the only noise coming from a few of the girls who are laughing between themselves about something. Olivia knows that whatever has happened or whatever joke has been shared, it is nothing that relates to her, and yet every titter she overhears, every smile on every happy face she happens to pass, feels like a sting, as though each student and every teacher finds amusement in her awkwardness and the gossip that has been spread around over these past few days.

Olivia has always believed that she has stood out, and she knows it has been for all the wrong reasons. Now, for the first time, she feels as though there's nothing more she wants than to continue to do just that.

'Right,' Miss Johnson says, commanding the attention of the class. 'Exam practice. We're just weeks away now, so the more of this we do now, the easier it'll be for you on the day. Story writing,' she says, introducing the topic by pointing to the whiteboard behind her. A few groans follow. 'Choose one of the titles from the board and write a plan as you would in the exam, please. You know by now what your story needs to include. No more than three characters, a clear beginning, middle and end, some dialogue where possible, and don't forget to add description. You've got five minutes.'

Most of the class lower their heads over their books, although when Olivia looks around her, there are some who are glancing down at their phones hidden beneath the desks and others who are staring blankly ahead, still clueless as to what they're supposed to be doing. Olivia's eyes rest on Miss Johnson, who has returned to her desk and is jotting something down in her teaching planner. She is wearing a dress today, knee-length with a belt that pulls in around her slim waist, and Olivia finds herself staring, wondering what the teacher's life is like beyond the four walls of this classroom.

She looks away when Miss Johnson glances up and catches her eye. Rather than say something, she looks back down as though she hasn't noticed. 'Three more minutes,' she says.

Olivia looks at the board. There are three titles to choose from: 'The Party'; 'A Bad Decision'; 'The Visitor'. Olivia already knows which one she will choose and what she will write; she can almost see her story writing itself in front of her without pen having yet been put to paper.

She picks up her biro and starts to write, ignoring the teacher's instruction to make a plan first. Moments later, Miss Johnson stops the class, but Olivia keeps writing, her brain working faster than her hand is possibly able to keep up with as the words flow onto the page. She knows she should be listening to whatever it is Miss Johnson is saying, but she doesn't want to stop now that she has started. She glances to her side, but the girl next to her pays her no attention, too busy picking at a split false nail. When Olivia looks up, she feels certain that the teacher must have noticed her not paying attention, but if she has, she says nothing. Olivia feels gratitude swell in her chest. It's almost as if she knows.

For the remaining forty minutes of the lesson, the class works in silence on their stories. At the end, Miss Johnson collects the work and puts it in a pile on her desk. When the bell sounds for lunch, the class is dismissed, but Olivia lingers near the doorway, waiting for everyone else to leave.

'Everything okay, Olivia?'

She nods and gestures to the pile of stories on the desk. 'Could you look at mine?'

Miss Johnson smiles. 'I'll take them home tonight and read them all by next lesson, okay?'

Olivia makes no attempt to conceal her disappointment and knows it is showing across her face. Miss Johnson must notice it, because she smiles again, this time as though trying to reassure her.

'Stop worrying,' she says. 'You work hard. You'll be fine.'

Olivia knows she's expected to be grateful for the comment, but she can't be. Beneath the school shirt that's suddenly too warm and too stiff, her heart is beating unbearably hard, and sweat is leaving her skin sticky against the polyester.

'What are you reading this week?' she asks, hearing the strange lilt in her own voice. She points to the book on the teacher's desk. Miss Johnson has told the class that she tries to read a book a week, sometimes bringing whatever she's reading to school with her to try to encourage the students. They've talked about the books before, though Olivia doubts that any of the conversations have ever made the students go and read them for themselves. More than likely these book-related chats have been nothing more than a way of delaying the lesson and eating into time working.

'It's quite a sad one this week,' Miss Johnson tells her. 'It's set during the Second World War. It's about a young couple who get separated and try to find each other.'

Olivia knows she is staring at her, but she can't help it. 'Do you like sad stories?'

Miss Johnson gives her a look that she's not quite able to read. She appears uncomfortable, her usual smile having fallen from her face and been replaced by something that makes her look awkward somehow. 'I like all types of stories. Right,' she says, glancing at the clock, 'you'd better get some lunch before all the best stuff's gone. I've got a meeting to get to. See you next week. I'm looking forward to reading what you've written.'

She manages to smile again, but Olivia is convinced that this one isn't genuine. She wonders what is going on in Miss Johnson's head, what she thinks of her right at that moment. She wants to say something else, but the words are trapped, and even if she could free them, she isn't sure they would make much sense, even to herself.

'Thanks,' she mutters, though she couldn't feel less thankful if she tried.

There is a whole weekend to pass until she sees Miss Johnson again, until she knows that she has read her story and will be able to see how she reacts to it. Olivia isn't sure she can wait that long.

Throwing her bag onto her shoulder, she leaves the classroom and heads downstairs. She leaves the humanities block and makes her way across the playground, heading towards the art block. What she is going to do has come to her like an epiphany, a moment of madness and triumph that she knows she must act upon now, quickly, before she has a chance to talk herself out of it.

The art block has a partial flat roof, which Olivia knows can be accessed from the back of the building. Students have got into trouble in the past for climbing up onto it, though it has never been properly blocked off to stop them from still doing so. She leaves her school bag on the concrete and climbs over the gate, making a poor effort and scraping the inside of her leg on a sharp prong of metal. She winces at the sight of blood bubbling to the surface of her pale skin, and at the stinging pain that follows.

Once beyond the railings, it is easy to make out the route that others have taken, and she pulls herself up onto the first ledge, cursing her lack of upper-body strength. Minimal exercise, frequent inertia and a lack of food have rendered her muscles useless; it takes all her effort and the power of her determination for her to make it to the top of the roof.

She makes her way to the far edge, which overlooks the main yard. Other students have started to filter out of the surrounding buildings, scurrying between blocks as they make their way to the canteen and various lunchtime clubs. She watches them like an outsider, as though these people are alien to her. For a moment, she closes her eyes. It feels disorientating, dizzying, yet just being up here is breathlessly exhilarating.

People have started to notice her. She can hear raised voices in the yard below, students calling one another, and when she opens her eyes, she sees them pointing to the roof to draw attention to her, not wanting anyone to miss out on whatever scene is about to unfold. It's higher than Olivia expected it to be. She feels like a bird, the people small and insignificant so far beneath her. She steps closer to the edge and peers down. The distance makes her dizzy and the air that circles around her seems so much stronger than it did just minutes earlier, with her feet on the ground.

'Olivia!'

She looks down, searching for the voice that has called her name. Among the crowd that has gathered is Mr Lewis, looking paler than Olivia has ever seen him. He puts a hand in front of him, his arm stretched high, as though he has a chance of pushing her back if she decides to jump now. She watches as he begins to dart between the students, hurrying to the main building to get help.

She allows her focus to rest on a few random faces in the crowd gathered below her. Some of them she recognises but doesn't know their names; others are familiar classmates who have contributed to making her life the hell that it has become. Phones have already come out from pockets, people desperate to catch what happens next on camera. She puts out a hand and waves, playing to her audience, then moves right to the edge of the roof, her toes pointing out over the drop. She closes her eyes and takes a deep breath.

THIRTEEN

HANNAH

'What the hell were you thinking?'

Olivia is sitting at the kitchen table, still dressed in her uniform. There is blood on her skirt, but Hannah hasn't yet got around to asking her about it. She doesn't even know whether it's Olivia's. She's starting to believe that nothing would surprise her any more.

She hasn't contacted Michael since receiving the phone call from the school; instead, she walked there to pick Olivia up, trying her best to ignore the expressions of the staff and the sniggers she heard from a few students who were lingering at the gates as they left. Their mirth might have related to some other subject, but Hannah doubts it. She remembers only too well what schools are like; gossip finds its way into every corner as soon as the act in question is complete. She doubts anything else could have happened that day to have earned the amount of attention Olivia has garnered.

Walking past that laughter, trying to ignore the comments whispered loud enough to be overheard, Hannah felt shame settle on her, clinging like a second skin, but Olivia seemed to breeze from the school grounds as though nothing had happened.

She is not her child, Hannah thinks. She finds it difficult to fathom how she could possibly have produced this girl who now sits in front of her, who has been capable of doing what Olivia has done. Her daughter has exposed herself to half the school, flaunting her bare chest from a rooftop overlooking the playground. It is the kind of thing that might appear in one of the trashy magazines her mother used to read; the type of story that makes other people feel better about their own disastrous lives. It isn't what Hannah ever imagined for her family, not after all she has done for them and the life they have been given. She has tried to bring her children up the right way, providing them with everything she herself never had. Though she knows she shouldn't take it as a personal affront, Olivia's behaviour feels like a punishment somehow, as though she is having all her efforts thrown back at her, disregarded and rejected.

After she received the phone call from Olivia's head of year and went to the school to collect her, Hannah and Olivia walked home in silence. There were a million and one things Hannah would have liked to say to her daughter, questions she still needs to ask but can't imagine that even Olivia will be able to find answers to. There is no plausible reason why she did what she did, not that Hannah can see anyway. Rather than face exposure to Olivia's prolonged silence, though, she kept the questions to herself. More than anything, it was pride that made her stay mute. She has never been the kind of woman to air her dirty laundry in public, and she's not going to be forced into it now by a wayward teen who seems intent on ruining the life she and Michael have built for themselves.

She allowed Olivia to go to her room when they got home, knowing that she needed time to calm down before she spoke to her. Now, a couple of hours later, her anger having had time to escalate and then subside, she stares at Olivia across the kitchen table, waiting for her to speak. When Olivia refuses to answer her, heat rises in her chest. She wants to scream, but she won't. Last night was the closest she has come in a long time to losing her patience, and she won't let it happen again. She would rather hold it all in than be reduced to wailing. Once that happens, she has lost control of the situation, and if there's one thing Hannah knows she must maintain here, it is some sort of control, as little as she feels she may have remaining.

'What you did today was shameful,' she says, trying to keep her voice steady. 'You've made a fool of yourself. You've embarrassed this family. What the hell do you think people are going to be saying about us after this?'

The smirk that crosses her daughter's face makes Hannah want to slap her. She has never done that. This is what Olivia wants, she thinks; she is trying to provoke her, desperate for a reaction, wanting her to resort to violence, because once she does that, Hannah has lost control. Olivia wins.

'I can't even look at you,' she says, crossing the kitchen and going to the window. She stands with her palms pressed on the rim of the sink and looks out onto the garden. Visions of Olivia as a five- or six-year-old flit in front of her, the ghost of the child she once was skipping on the lawn, innocently engrossed with the task of not tripping on the rope as it swung back to the ground. Hannah feels the loss like a pain in her chest, gripping at her heart, yet there is something else too, something she has tried for years to ignore and has never known how to name. Perhaps Olivia was never that little girl, not really; not beneath the surface. Maybe Hannah saw what she chose to see, desperate to avoid a far uglier truth.

'People will have filmed it on their phones, you realise that, don't you? You're probably halfway across the internet by now.'

She hasn't had a chance to look yet; she doesn't know if she can bring herself to do it. She has heard of these things before, of stories about young girls who have allowed their boyfriends to photograph or film them in ways they wouldn't want their parents to know about, only to find when the relationship sours that their exes have shared the images with their friends online. And not just their friends, Hannah thinks. Once something is up on social media, it's there for anyone to see. Already it might be the case that strange men have been ogling her teenage daughter's bare chest, using the images to encourage all manner of fantasies. The thought makes her feel sick.

'Go to your room,' she says, without turning to look at Olivia. She is so angry, she doesn't know how she can deal with her from here. She hasn't wanted to admit that Michael might be better equipped to cope with Olivia's recent behaviour, not having wanted to seem like a failure, but now she realises that the decision about her future lies with him, and that everything he has said to Hannah previously might be right. 'Your father will decide what happens next.'

She listens to Olivia leave without protest and head upstairs, hopeful that for once she will do as she is told. Olivia is headstrong and unruly, but she must know she has taken things too far. The vandalism of the house at the weekend … the call from Rosie's school … and now this. Hannah still doesn't want to admit it aloud, but she knows her daughter is out of control. She wears it well, assuming an appearance of normality, but it is obvious that she is harbouring a darkness that has yet to be fully seen. Hannah has failed her by not being able to keep the darkness from them all, and yet she believes that even had she done things differently, where Olivia is concerned the outcome would have been the same. This is more than nurture. Olivia is a product of something else entirely.

Where do they go from here? she thinks. They can't ground her; what effect would that have? Michael will know – Michael already knows – and yet the thought of telling him what Olivia has done now fills Hannah with so much dread it makes her feel nauseous. Their life as they have known it until now is going to be ripped apart. It is exactly what Olivia has been trying to achieve.

She goes to the hallway and retrieves her mobile phone from her jacket pocket. When she tries Michael's mobile, it goes straight to the answerphone. She knows the name of the hotel where he is staying that evening; she always makes sure that she knows where he is in case there's an emergency and she can't get hold of him. She searches the internet for the hotel phone number, taps it into her mobile and waits for an answer. When someone picks up, she asks if she can speak to a guest called Michael Walters.

There is a pause. 'I'm sorry,' the man says. 'There's no one of that name staying here this evening.'

Hannah apologises, not really knowing why she does so, and ends the call. Her heart has slowed a little and a headache is pulsing behind her eyes, blurring her vision. Where is he? She knows that he's got a lot on, but she needs him here. If he can't be with her, he should at least make himself available at the end of the phone. If he's not at that hotel, then where is he staying? And why has he lied to her about where he is tonight?

She feels tears spike at the corners of her eyes, hot and sudden. She wipes them away, embarrassed by their appearance despite there being no one else to witness them. She feels gripped by isolation, suffocated by it, yet this feeling is nothing new. She has experienced it since she was a child, finding ways to make her loneliness more bearable. With Michael, she never thought she would feel this way. She has a beautiful home; she is blessed with children … This life is everything she ever wanted. It was until recently, at least. Olivia's silence and her increasingly difficult behaviour are spoiling what would otherwise be a blissful existence. And yet even without the drama of these past few days, contentment hasn't reached her yet. She wonders whether she is just ungrateful. Is she being punished for not fully appreciating everything she has? Does the fault lie with her?

She tries Michael's mobile again, but once again it goes straight to answerphone. She waits for the beep, but when the chance to speak comes, she finds herself saying nothing. She cuts the call, leaving him to be met with silence when he next checks his messages. A part of her hopes it will come across as ominous as it sounds.

She watches television for a while, not really paying attention to anything that plays out in front of her. At just before 10 p.m. she goes upstairs and gets ready for bed, not bothering to check on either of the girls as she usually does. She falls into sleep quickly, but it is dream-filled and restless. She is too hot, too cold, too preoccupied with everything the past week has thrown at her. After an hour of tossing and turning, of fighting the duvet off only to pull it up around her neck again, she drifts into a deeper sleep, where her dreams are vivid and alive, taking her to places she would never willingly allow herself to return to.

There is a man in the darkness; she hasn't seen him, but she can sense that he is there. He is standing over her, his boots on the soft mud that she is lying in. She can feel the cold wetness of the ground seeping through her clothing, chilling her to the naked skin beneath her dress. She can't see properly, not just because of the darkness but because of something else, something that hurts her head and stings behind her eyes.

She feels a hand on her shoulder, and it rips her from the dream. 'Hannah.'

'Christ,' she says, putting a hand to her chest. 'Don't do that, Michael – you could have given me a heart attack.'

She turns over beneath the duvet, her eyes adjusting to the shapes within the darkened room. Her husband is lying on the bed beside her, his coat still on. She catches his smile among the shadows.

'I thought I'd surprise you.'

'Well you certainly did that.' Hannah pushes herself up and sits back against the pillows. 'Haven't you looked at your phone? I've been trying to get hold of you.'

'Sorry, love. Been driving, haven't checked it. It's probably still on silent from the meeting earlier.' His eyes meet hers in the darkness. 'What's the matter?'

'I called the hotel. They said no one called Michael Walters was staying there today.'

'I decided to come home. I thought you'd be happy to see me.'

She is, but for all the wrong reasons, ones she knows are selfish and preoccupied with the hope of making her own life easier. She doesn't want to have to deal with Olivia alone, and she hopes that Michael will take the burden of finding a way to resolve the situation from her. Where Olivia is concerned, Hannah isn't convinced a resolution can be found, and yet she knows already that Michael has a plan. She is just waiting to see whether he will follow it through.

'I am. Why didn't they just tell me you'd cancelled your room then?'

'Christ, Hannah, I don't know,' he says, standing and slipping off his shoes. 'I'd probably been taken off the system by the time you called.' He removes his coat and hangs it on the hook on the back of the bedroom door. 'Why do I feel as though I'm being interrogated?'

Hannah sits up, leans over and turns on the bedside lamp. Michael is unbuttoning his work shirt. He looks tired, as always – heavy shadows sit beneath his eyes and he's in need of a shave – and she feels guilty for giving him such a hard time. What happened today is not his fault. Despite the thoughts that flitted through her mind earlier, neither of them is to blame for this.

'I'm sorry.'

'What's happened, anyway?' he asks, removing his trousers and returning to the bed.

'Nothing,' she lies. The thought of what happened that afternoon crashes down on top of her, sleep having briefly removed the weight of it from her consciousness. She thinks of the internet, of her daughter's body being shared on social media, and tries to push the images away from the front of her mind. She doesn't know how she is going to tell Michael about the shame their daughter has brought upon the family. She has no idea how he might react. 'It's Olivia,' she says, her voice small.

'Is she okay?'

'Yes, but—'

'Good,' Michael says, cutting her short. 'She's safe and well, then?'

Hannah nods. 'The thing is—'

He puts a finger to her lips, silencing her. His fingertips are cold with the lingering chill of the night air, and she feels a shiver snake through her, pushing goose bumps up on her flesh.

'Whatever it is, Hannah, can it wait until tomorrow, please? Just this once, let's have a night without drama, shall we?'

When he kisses her, Hannah responds with more enthusiasm than she knows she has shown him in a long time, forcing herself into a reciprocation that doesn't come naturally to her, not when she is so preoccupied by everything else. She knows he is right; they deserve some peace and some happiness. Not everything can be about Olivia, regardless of her intent to make it so.

Michael lifts her T-shirt and she allows him to take it off without resistance. He moves towards her, his bare chest hot against hers, and when he pushes her to the bed, she sinks into the mattress beneath the weight of him, happy to have his body smother hers; grateful in this moment that at least she can be distracted from thoughts of her daughter. When he pulls away and pushes himself up on his arms, Hannah thinks he has changed his mind. Instead, he leans over and switches her bedside lamp off, submerging them back into darkness.

She closes her eyes and waits for the sex to pass, going through the motions in the way she knows is expected of her. She wishes she could feel something, something more, but she is detached from herself and from her body, as though she is looking down upon them both, senseless and unfeeling. When he is done, Michael rolls off her, kisses her shoulder and turns his back to her; before long, she is listening to the heavy breathing of his deep sleep. Knowing she won't find peace for herself for quite some time yet, Hannah lies in the darkness and cries silent tears.

FOURTEEN

OLIVIA

Olivia lies in bed trying to listen out for sound. Any sound will do, just something to break the monotony of the long hours she has spent here in silence, lying alone and trying not to think too hard about what has happened and what might happen next as a consequence. Her legs feel deadened, pinned to the bed, and she longs for sleep, for the break it would allow her from the relentless circling of her thoughts. It felt liberating being up on that roof, a kind of freedom she has never experienced before. She knows that what she did was stupid, but everyone else her age seems to get away with doing stupid things. For everyone else, recklessness seems to be a rite of passage, gift-wrapped with the gloss of youth, yet for her the rules have always seemed to be different. She isn't allowed to make mistakes or to learn from experience. She must do as they say, and not as they do.

She knows the people in her year who have had sex already, as well as the ones who have taken drugs. She knows which of them go out and get drunk in parks at the weekend and which of them have been in trouble with the police. There's a girl in the sixth form who's rumoured to have had an affair with one of the teaching assistants, an affair apparently everyone but his girlfriend knows about. The other staff must know – the rumour mill went into meltdown with it back before Christmas – yet the teaching assistant still works at the school, with no repercussions for whatever he's been getting up to. The same for the student, who'll be leaving school in just a few weeks' time. What Olivia did yesterday was nothing in comparison to other people's antics, yet she already knows that she will pay a higher price for it than any of her classmates would.

The thought of being stuck in this house and in this room any longer is enough to drive her insane. Some days she believes she might already be mad. Her thoughts are erratic and disjointed, and quite often she thinks things she isn't sure are normal. She tries not to linger on them, but sometimes the more attempts she makes to avoid these thoughts that plague her, the harder they hit, each time darker and more distressing. She wonders what it would be like to be allowed access to the brain of another person, for just ten minutes or so, to know if the way she thinks is typical or if other people are wired differently to her. Would it be a good thing? she wonders. Knowing she's not that unlike someone else might offer a reassurance she's aware she is in desperate need of, but finding out she's irredeemably more different would push her even further towards an invisible edge she finds herself crawling closer to by the day. Perhaps ignorance really is bliss, and yet Olivia knows this not to be the case. She has been ignorant for long enough.

If her mother thinks she will start talking to her because they are forced together inside this house, then she is mistaken; Olivia has come this far and she's not going to back down now. She knows she is going to be suspended, that much is certain. She has never really broken school rules before – no crime greater than forgetting to underline the date at the top of her exercise book – but she knows that flashing your tits from the school roof crosses the boundaries of what the head teacher will regard as acceptable. She'll be surprised if she's punished with anything more than suspension, not when only last year, Patrick Backley from year nine sliced another boy's arm with a broken test tube he'd taken from one of the science labs, and was back in school the following week. She thinks she would have to do something really extreme to be expelled.

She smiles as she recalls the looks on some of the faces below her as she pulled her shirt over her head. She knew that they were expecting her to jump. It's always the quiet ones, that's what they say, isn't it? She's pretty sure that removing her bra was the last thing anyone expected her to do, and the feeling of shocking people, of doing something completely out of character, is one she isn't able to put into words. She has always stood out, but this time she could do so on her own terms.

Her mother is right about the internet, of course. She hadn't allowed herself to dwell too deeply on it beforehand; if she had, she knows she might have talked herself out of it. Anyway, she wasn't thinking too much about anything; everything happened so quickly. The idea came so suddenly that she knew she would have to do it there and then, or risk losing the moment of opportunity. Now, thinking about the fact that it will almost certainly have reached the internet by now, her smile fades. She wonders what is being said about her. After Friday, people were already whispering about her, speaking words that just two weeks ago no one might have imagined they would ever use to describe Olivia Walters. Now, she can only guess at the comments.

But she doesn't care. It will all be worth it, she feels sure of it.

She wonders whether Miss Johnson has read her story yet. Perhaps hearing about what happened at lunchtime might have prompted her into looking at it sooner than she had planned, though Olivia isn't sure why that might be the case. She wishes now that she had spoken to Miss Johnson while she had the chance. She has tried to make herself noticeable to her, but their last exchange might only have resulted in her coming across as even weirder than people already think her. Perhaps she could have told her about Friday and what happened at the party, about everything that's been going on. Maybe the consequences wouldn't have been as bad as she feared. If anyone would understand, she feels certain it would be Miss Johnson. She's young, she's female ... Olivia imagines that she gets all this. She thinks she's probably still aware of what it means to be young, in ways that her mother has long since lost and might never have been in possession of at all. She should have just confided in the teacher while she had the opportunity. After everything else, it doesn't feel as though things can get any worse. Either way, the chance has gone now, and Olivia mourns it like a lost friend.

She wonders once again about Miss Johnson's life. She does this quite a lot, picturing her as she might appear outside of school, in her home or out running. She knows that Miss Johnson enters races; she has talked to the class about running half-marathons to raise money for charity. She is currently training for a triathlon, and Olivia wonders if she swims in the sea for practice, maybe down by the pier where she herself stood earlier that week.

She knows that Miss Johnson isn't married, but she doesn't know whether she has a boyfriend. In her imaginings, the teacher's life is like something from a Hollywood film. She wears beautiful clothes with designer labels and eats in fancy restaurants that have menus on which half the items can only be pronounced by the waiters; she goes on dates with handsome men, but she doesn't need any of them, not if she decides she doesn't like them enough. She is sophisticated and independent, everything Olivia would like one day to be. Miss Johnson doesn't have to do what she is told. She can do whatever she likes, whenever she likes.

Olivia has never really known what it's like to have a friend – no one comes to the house, and she has never grown close to anyone at school – but if she ever has one, she hopes it will be someone like Miss Johnson, someone uncomplicated and happy; someone she can trust with her secrets.

As her eyes grow heavier and her thoughts become cloudier, she drifts into sleep, the dream of a different life following her there. She is standing barefoot on a beach. It is night-time and the tide is out, and the wet sand has oozed between her toes. It is cold and breezy, but she doesn't care. The noise of the wind fills her ears and the smell that the sea has left lingers in the air around her, and on the tip of her tongue is the taste of the night, as though all her senses have been wakened by just being there, in this spot that she's never seen.

She is woken by the sound of her bedroom door. She has always been a light sleeper, roused by the noise of a creaking floorboard or a hushed voice on the landing. She lies facing the wall and waits with her eyes open, her back to whoever has entered the room. She flinches as the duvet is pulled back and a stream of cold air hits the bare skin of her neck.

'Olivia.' Rosie's voice is small in the darkness. She climbs onto the bed beside her sister, making too much noise as she tries to rearrange the duvet to cover herself.

'What do you want?'

'I just wanted to see if you're okay.'

'I'm fine. Or I was until you came in here and stole all the duvet.' Olivia yanks it back, getting twisted up in it as she turns to tickle her sister's ribs. 'You're not supposed to be in here.' She says it in a whisper, pulling her hand away before Rosie's giggles become too loud and disturb the quiet that rests over the house.

Rosie's eyes meet hers in the darkness. 'Mum told me what happened. She said she wanted me to hear it from her before I found out about it from someone else.'

Olivia sighs and waits for what might come next. Rosie loves an opportunity to reprimand her, as though she is the older sister and knows anything about anything. Usually her matronly lectures are a regurgitation of things their mother has said; anything to help her make herself feel superior. Olivia wonders why she feels the need to prove herself, when it is Rosie who already has the upper hand in everything: she is more loved, more accepted, more normal than Olivia believes she is capable of ever being.

Instead of the expected lecture, Rosie starts to giggle. She stifles the sound by putting a hand across her mouth. 'Did you really show half the school your boobies?'

'Boobies?'

And now both girls are laughing, smothering the noise by putting their heads under the duvet, their shoulders shaking as they try to calm themselves.

'Stop it now,' Olivia says, knowing how much trouble they will both be in if they wake their parents.

'Why did you do it?' Rosie asks, once her snickering has finally subsided.

Olivia shifts onto her side to face her. She can feel the warmth of her sister's body, and she wants to wrap an arm around her, comfort herself with the heat that pulses from her small form. 'I've got really good boobies,' she says, gently mocking. 'I thought people deserved to see them.'

In the darkness, she can see that Rosie isn't impressed with the response. 'You're on the internet.'

Olivia raises an eyebrow and attempts a smile. 'Job done then,' she says lightly, though inside she feels anything but light-hearted. How can she explain why she did it? Sometimes she can barely explain how she feels to herself. 'Do you ever feel different to other people?' she asks.

Rosie pulls a face. 'Sometimes, I suppose.'

Olivia's eyes widen. They have adjusted to the darkness now, and she can see her sister's red hair sticking out from behind her ears; the tiny crusts of sleep stuck in the corners of her eyes. She has a series of lines along one side of her face where she has been sleeping on a crumpled pillow.

'Come on, Rosie. I mean, really different.' She stares at her sister, willing her to look back, this time properly. They lie like this for a moment, the silence deafening them with all the things they cannot say aloud. Rosie doesn't speak, but she nods, the gesture enough to tell Olivia everything she needs to know.

For so long she has thought Rosie hates her, but she doesn't, she understands that now. They need each other. She puts an arm out and beckons her sister closer, pulling her into a hug. Rosie lies in the crook of her arm, her head resting against Olivia's hair. Before long, she has fallen asleep there, and Olivia breathes in the scent of her sister's red curls, wishing they could be lying together somewhere else: a white-sand beach or a field filled with buttercups, only the sky above them and nothing but the noise of the birds and the breeze. She listens to the rise and fall of her sister's breathing, thinking how lovely it would be if they could stay like that until morning.

'Rosie.' She shakes her sister by the shoulder, rousing her. 'Go back to your room now.'

In a sleep-filled state, Rosie pulls herself from Olivia's embrace and gets up from the bed. Then she says something Olivia doesn't think they've ever said to each other before, or if they have, it was so long ago that she can no longer remember it.

'Love you.'

In the darkness, Olivia smiles sadly. 'Night, Rosie. Love you too.'

FIFTEEN
HANNAH

When Hannah wakes on Thursday morning, Michael is already showered, dressed and downstairs. He is wearing his work clothes and drinking a coffee at the kitchen table, scrolling through his phone with his free hand. A lump of bile lodges in Hannah's throat at the thought of what he might be looking at, but when he puts the phone on the table and greets her with a casual good morning, she knows he hasn't seen or heard what she has feared he might have.

Her husband looks happy this morning, his good humour no doubt encouraged by what happened between them last night. Hannah hates that she is going to have to kill that happiness, but she knows she must; if he hears about it elsewhere, he will be furious with her for having said nothing.

'Last night ...' she says, going to the table and sitting beside him.

'Good, wasn't it?'

'Not that. I wanted to tell you something, something about Olivia.'

'Have you seen her this morning?'

Hannah shakes her head. 'She can stay in her room. I've got to be at the school at eleven thirty, for a meeting with the head. Something happened yesterday.'

Michael is looking at her intently, waiting for her to continue. Hannah feels suddenly self-conscious in the T-shirt and shorts she's still wearing. She wishes now that she had showered first, got dressed into something more appropriate, though she isn't sure what difference either of these things would have made.

'Hannah? What happened?'

She takes her phone from the pocket of her shorts and plays him one of the clips that has been shared online, turning her head away so that she doesn't have to expose herself to yet another viewing of her daughter's shameful actions. There is no point in trying to hide anything from him; he is going to find out anyway. She glances at his face, but he is giving away nothing, his expression impassive as he watches the footage to its end. When it finishes, she returns the phone to her pocket. She sees Michael's jaw tauten in the first sign of a reaction.

'I thought for a minute she was going to jump,' he says quietly.

Hannah nods. 'I think everyone did.' She puts her elbows on the table and her head in her hands. 'What are we going to do, Michael? The house, the phone call from Rosie's school, now this. She's out of control, isn't she?'

If she is being punished, it has gone far enough. Perhaps she should have told Michael the truth about the argument on Friday evening. Maybe he could have dealt with the situation more effectively than she has been able to, and yesterday's incident might have been avoided. Either way, Hannah realises it is too late for that. If she tells him the truth now, it will only make things worse.

Michael stands, his chair scraping noisily across the tiled floor of the kitchen.

'Where are you going?' Hannah asks, her voice panicked.

'I'm just going to speak to her. I want to hear her side of things.'

Hannah waits in the kitchen. Michael closes the door behind him, and she listens to his footsteps on the stairs as he heads to Olivia's room. She glances at the clock. There are hours to kill before she needs to leave the house to go to the school, time she knows will seem long and arduous. It means yet another morning spent overthinking and trying – and failing – to avoid what is out there on the internet.

Knowing she shouldn't, but unable to resist the urge that makes her return to it, she takes her phone back out of her pocket and goes to the footage of Olivia once again. Her daughter's public display of indecency has been shared by numerous students, each short clip depicting a different angle of her shame. Hannah laments the state of the world they live in. Rather than trying to get to Olivia to stop her doing whatever she was planning, people were far more interested in reaching for their phones and recording the moment so they could later torment her with the living memory of it. She imagines that those who have shared the footage have gained followers by doing so, using Olivia's behaviour to benefit their own narcissism. There was a time when Hannah would have prided herself on the fact that her children would never behave in such a way, but after this past week, she feels as though anything is possible. Olivia is impossible to predict, and Hannah knows now that that is dangerous.

She turns the sound down on her phone and plays the first clip. The filming is shaky, the phone held up in unsteady hands, but the job is good enough to capture everything Hannah doesn't want the world to see. Olivia stands at the edge of the roof, peering at the ground below. It looks as though she is going to jump, and the collective gasp that swells from the waiting crowd when she takes a step forward is evidence that they expected the same, a fact that only serves to makes the filming of the incident even more sickening. Had her daughter wanted to kill herself, there were people there who would have filmed it, played it back, shared it.

There are raised voices in the background, people shouting, then a series of jeers and wolf whistles as Olivia reaches for the hem of her school shirt and pulls it up over her head in one swift movement. Cheers follow, then laughter. The filming becomes jerkier as the person holding the phone laughs along with the rest of the braying crowd. Hannah watches with shame and horror as her daughter puts her hands behind her back, unclips her bra and whips it away from her body in the manner of some cheap nightclub stripper, leaving her in only her skirt and her shoes. The bra is thrown behind her, landing somewhere out of sight on the roof.

Hannah stops the video; she can't bear to watch any more. She scrolls to the comments below, her heart throbbing at the things she sees written there.

SkyGirl03
WTF was she thinking??!
AmyLou
Always knew this girl was nuts
DanDan2002
State of it – got tits like my nan
CallumJay
Why you seen your nan's rack? Perv
Westie
Sucks on them titties when she puts him to bed
StaceyJones
Loooooooooool
DanDan2002
Fuck you Westie haha

Hannah can't read any more; she is disgusted by it all: the language, the coarseness, the things they are saying about Olivia. She is angry with these people she has never even seen before, yet she knows what she feels towards them can't compare with the way she feels towards her daughter. She slams her phone down on the table and sits in silence, listening out for any sound from upstairs. There is none. She tries to imagine what Michael might be saying to Olivia, but she has no idea how he is taking all this.

She busies herself with anything that comes to hand, putting away the few dishes that stand on the draining rack from the night before and rotating the food in the fridge so that the items with the closest use-by dates are nearest the front of the shelves. When she's finished this, she starts taking tins and packets from the cupboards, wiping the shelves below before returning the contents.

A while later, Michael returns. He has been upstairs for nearly half an hour. She wants to ask him what happened, yet at the same time she doesn't want to know.

'I need to get to work,' he tells her. There is no mention of Olivia or what has been said; whether she even spoke to him this time.

'Is everything okay?'

'I'm going to be late.'

With that, he brings the conversation to an end, making it clear that whatever went on upstairs, he wishes it to remain between Olivia and him. She tells him quietly that she will see him later.

After he leaves the house, she goes upstairs and stands on the landing outside Olivia's bedroom, her ear pressed to the closed door. She waits, listens harder; she hears her daughter's sobs, soft and suppressed. She thinks about going into the room, but stops herself. It is likely she will only be met with silence. Instead, she showers and gets dressed, choosing an outfit appropriate for her forthcoming meeting with the head teacher. She needs to make the right impression; it is her responsibility now to try to counteract everything that Olivia has suggested about their family through her recent behaviour.

Before she leaves for the school, Hannah makes a sandwich and pours a glass of orange juice. She sets them on a tray with a couple of biscuits and carries the tray up to Olivia's room. Her daughter is in bed, her back turned to the room. Hannah knows she isn't sleeping, but she doesn't turn to acknowledge her mother when she enters the room.

She sets the tray down on the bedside table. 'Try to eat something.' She finds herself unable to say any more, still furious with Olivia for what she's done.

Half an hour later, Hannah is being escorted by the school receptionist to the head teacher's office. She has seen the head teacher before, though she has never needed to speak with her, and as she is led into her office, she feels grateful that there is no one else in the corridor to witness her shame.

'Mrs Parker,' she says quickly, as the head gestures to one of the chairs waiting near her desk. 'I'm so sorry for Olivia's behaviour. I don't know what possessed her.'

The head sits down and puts her hands on the desk top. 'We're all surprised by what happened yesterday, Mrs Walters. It's just so out of character – I don't think Olivia's been in any sort of trouble in the five years she's been here. I don't remember her even attending an after-school detention.'

Hannah shakes her head, not knowing what to say. She doesn't want to be here; she shouldn't have to be here. She wishes Michael was beside her, yet she also doubts his being there would be such a good idea. He was furious when he came downstairs after seeing Olivia earlier; he didn't need to say anything to make his anger known.

'Has she told you why she did it?'

Hannah shakes her head. She's not going to volunteer anything this woman doesn't need to know, not when the fact that there is an ongoing argument will only add suspicion to what is already strange enough behaviour. Telling the head teacher that Olivia hasn't spoken to her in almost a week isn't going to help matters, and she won't allow her daughter to implicate her and Michael in the way she might be hoping to. This is on Olivia, all of it, and she will have to deal with the repercussions.

'I'm sorry to have to ask,' Mrs Parker says, 'but is everything okay at home?'

Hannah resents the question and the implications that come with it, and the look that passes across Mrs Parker's face says she has noticed the immediate offence she has taken. 'Everything is fine,' she says, a little more bluntly than she intends. She sighs and looks down at her hands in her lap. 'This is as much a shock to us as it is to you.'

'Has anything happened that might have prompted the behaviour, do you think?'

Hannah shakes her head. 'Like I said, it has come completely out of nowhere.' She looks Mrs Parker in the eye. 'I'll be honest with you – Olivia's behaviour has been challenging recently. She's always been a good girl, but at the moment she seems to be doing everything she can to test her father and me. Maybe it's her age, I don't know. I certainly don't know why she did what she did. I can only assure you that it most definitely won't happen again.'

Mrs Parker nods slowly, but she is looking at Hannah as though this is in some way her fault. 'A few of Olivia's teachers have commented on her recent weight loss. I'm sure you've discussed it with her at home.'

'She's a teenage girl,' Hannah says defensively, knowing her tone is only likely to exacerbate the tension between them. 'You know what they're like at this age; all about image.'

'Of course. We're just a little concerned that it's happened so quickly in her case.'

Hannah squeezes the fingers of her right hand in her lap until her knuckles whiten. 'Olivia was always slightly overweight as a child. She's lost weight, yes, but she's probably healthier now than she was this time last year.'

Mrs Parker gives her a look that Hannah chooses not to analyse. This is none of the woman's business, and she has no right to sit here questioning Hannah, making her feel as though she's inadequate as a parent.

'Okay. Look, I'm sorry to have to do this, I really am, but I have no choice other than to suspend Olivia for a week.'

Hannah nods; she knew that this was inevitable. She is angrier with Olivia than she has ever been, at having done such a stupid and shameful thing, and at having done it so close to the start of her GCSE exams. It feels as though she has timed it purposely, as though she has waited until now in order to wreak as much devastation as she can. She is punishing herself, if only she would see it, but she is too headstrong and too defiant to be told any different.

As though reading her thoughts, Mrs Parker says, 'I'm assuming Olivia will be back for the last few weeks before her exams start?'

'Of course.' Hannah pushes her chair back and stands. She doesn't know what else can be said, and she wants nothing more now than to be away from this room. She didn't come here to be judged, though she feels this is exactly what is happening. The look stamped on the head teacher's face is enough to confirm that she believes Hannah to be a failure as a mother; Hannah imagines that the woman had condemned her before she even entered the room. She feels deflated, defeated, knowing that her parenting has been thrown into question, knowing that this is exactly what Olivia wants. That her daughter is winning.

SIXTEEN

OLIVIA

Olivia is still in bed, still staring at the wall. The one-sided conversation her father had with her plays over in her head, taunting her. *Shameful … embarrassment …* These words are nothing new; she has heard them all from her mother. The rest, though, those were things she hadn't been expecting. She wonders whether her mother knows of her father's plans. Perhaps they aren't real, she tells herself, desperately clinging to the hopeless notion that his threat might be nothing more than just that.

Would it be so bad if he really means it? she thinks. Perhaps it would be a blessing in disguise, a chance for her to do the things she's always wanted. Her father used it as a threat, but what if he is giving her an opportunity of a lifetime? She would be free from this place, at least; free from her parents' nagging and their incessant rules.

She can hope all she wants, but the possibility that it might turn out to be a good thing is a distant prospect. Her father wouldn't plan something without knowing exactly how it will play out; he is far too meticulous and clever for that. They want her to be punished for what she has done, for whatever it is they are worried about her doing next, and there is still a part of her that wonders whether she deserves all this. Perhaps there really is something wrong with her, just as so many other people have told her over the years.

She tries to sleep, but she has already slept more than she needs to, and she cannot return to it, not while there is so much to think about. She knows her mother has been to the school to discuss her punishment, and she wonders what has been said about her there. She shouldn't care, and yet she does. People already think all sorts about her. She has been called more names than she is able to remember, so what will a few more matter now? What matters is what happens next, and the uncertainty of the future fills Olivia was a sickening fear that makes her feel worse than she has ever felt before.

She is considering her father's threat when there is a small tapping at her bedroom door and Rosie's head appears, her red hair pulled into a flowing ponytail that sits upon her left shoulder. She looks grown up, Olivia thinks, too grown up, and the thought fills her with a hope that until now she might have easily believed could never exist. It won't be like this forever, she reminds herself. Neither of them will be children forever, and when they are adults, they will be able to do as they please.

'Are you okay?' Rosie climbs into the bed and wraps her arms around her sister.

Olivia wants to cry, so she does, hot tears burning her eyes and streaking her face. She doesn't answer the question; she doesn't need to. She can't remember the last time she was okay.

'Where's Mum?' she asks, wiping a hand over her eyes. She already feels bad for getting upset in front of Rosie. She's the older sister; she should be the stronger of the two.

'On the phone.'

The girls tighten their embrace, knowing the call is likely to be short and that their time together will be ended when their mother's conversation is over.

'If I tell you something, do you promise not to mention it to Mum or Dad?'

Rosie nods.

'I mean it, Rosie. This is serious, okay? You can't say anything about it, not to them or anyone else.'

'What is it?' Rosie looks worried now.

'Dad wants to send me away.'

Rosie's mouth falls open, but no sound escapes her. The girls sit in silence for a moment.

Rosie is the first to speak. 'But why?'

Olivia shrugs, feigning ignorance. She knows exactly why he wants to send her away, but she's still not sure that Rosie is old enough or aware enough to understand. 'They think I'm out of control.'

'You've done some weird stuff recently.' Rosie sniffs and runs the back of her hand across her eyes. She tries to stifle a sob, but the noise is louder than she had intended, and Olivia feels it in her chest like the force of a fist. 'I don't want them to send you away.'

Both girls are crying now. Rosie's nose is running, and she wipes it on the sleeve of her school jumper. 'Send you away to where?' she says eventually. 'And why? I still don't understand.'

Olivia pauses, unsure whether she should answer every question Rosie has. She doesn't fully understand these places herself, only that wayward, troublesome teenagers are sent there to be rehabilitated before their behaviour becomes worse. Maybe Rosie is better off not knowing anything about it, and yet Olivia knows she needs her. Rosie is all she has.

'You don't know what happened here at the weekend, do you?'

Rosie shakes her head.

'On Saturday night, someone broke into the house. I'm not sure exactly what happened, but they smashed the back door. Mum and Dad have been really weird since it happened.'

'Did they take anything?'

'I don't know. They might have heard me on the stairs and left before they got a chance, but …' Olivia trails into silence, not believing her own words. Whoever was here on Saturday, it was something more personal. Someone wanted to unnerve them, to make them feel unsafe. She just doesn't know who, or why. 'They think it was me,' she says eventually.

Rosie pulls a face. 'Why would they think it was you? Why would you do that?'

'I don't know.' It's not quite true. She doesn't know exactly why, but she feels that whatever happened here at the weekend might have something to do with her grandmother. She has considered the possibility of telling Rosie about her – about this woman who until the previous week Olivia had believed to be dead – but it doesn't seem fair to do that to her, not now. There is enough going on to confuse her already; she doesn't need to be exposed to any more complications.

Olivia is confused herself. She doesn't know how or why a break-in at their house might link back to a woman too frail to leave her care-home bedroom without assistance, but what she does know is that things have started to change here, some silent shift that hasn't yet made itself visible but is being felt already, by her and by her parents. They sense it coming, she knows they do. They are fearful of it, and the notion makes Olivia feel unusually empowered.

She has wondered if her mother knows that she went to the care home to see Eleanor. Someone there might have told her that Olivia had been there, or what if Eleanor herself told Hannah that her daughter had been to visit her? If either of these things has happened, her mother has said nothing to her about it.

'Who could have been here?' Rosie asks quietly, and Olivia feels a pang of guilt at having scared her now, unsettling her in the only place she has ever been able to call home. She doesn't want her to go to bed tonight feeling afraid of intruders, though she doesn't want her to be complacent either. Rosie needs to know that the world they live in is a fragile one, dangerous, and that it is due to collapse around their ears any day now.

'I don't know. I only know it wasn't me. And you know that phone call from your school, the one Mum got saying you'd been in an accident? They think that was me as well.'

'But why would you do that?' Rosie asks, her voice becoming higher and more agitated with every question.

'Well I wouldn't, would I? *We* know that, but they obviously don't.'

Rosie's little face contorts as she tries to make sense of everything she's been told. 'Why would someone want Mum to think I'd been in an accident?'

'I don't know,' Olivia admits again, hating the fact that she knows so little. She feels more responsible for Rosie now than she ever has in her life. It is her duty to protect her, and that's exactly what she's going to do.

'Where does Dad want to send you?'

'To some sort of summer boot camp, the type they have in America for naughty kids.' She hears her father's words repeat in her ear: *respect … morals … discipline.* He wants her gone, but Olivia doesn't believe for a second it's for the reasons he is claiming.

'I need you to do something for me, Rosie. I need you to go into Mum's room and look for a diary. It's red; looks like an old exercise book.'

Rosie looks horrified at the suggestion. 'Why don't you do it?'

Olivia raises an eyebrow. 'I can't, can I? She won't trust me being in there, but if she sees you, she won't be so angry, will she?'

Rosie takes a moment to consider Olivia's reasoning. 'What excuse am I supposed to make?' she asks, wiping her eyes.

Their parents' bedroom has always been out of bounds, ever since they were small. Their mother argued that it was the only child-free room in the house, and that they deserved to have a space that wasn't littered with the clutter that comes with childhood.

'I don't know,' Olivia says, her frustration mounting. 'Tell her you need something for school, just think of anything. Please, Rosie. I need you to do this for me. It's so important. Please.'

Rosie sighs and rubs her hand across her face. 'What if I get in trouble too?'

'You won't, I promise. Their bedroom is so tidy, there's not that many places to hide a diary. You're a smart girl, Rosie, you can do this.'

Rosie smiles at the compliment; they aren't handed out often, not by Olivia. She wipes the last of her tears away and nods, a silent agreement that she will do as her sister requests.

'I don't want them to send you away.'

Olivia reaches out to Rosie, pulls her close and kisses her on the forehead. 'Don't worry,' she tells her. 'I'm not going anywhere.'

SEVENTEEN

HANNAH

'Mum,' Rosie says. 'Could you help me with this homework, please?'

Hannah is unloading plates from the dishwasher while her daughter sits behind her, her schoolbooks covering the kitchen table. 'Just give me a minute.' She finishes what she's doing before joining Rosie, scanning the opened page she is studying. It is a maths problem involving a delayed train and passengers who are going to be late for work.

'You've gone wrong here, by the looks of things,' Hannah says, pointing a finger to a section of Rosie's calculations. 'That should be ten, not a hundred.'

Rosie tuts. 'Silly me.' She takes her eraser and rubs out the mistake, replacing it with the correct number. 'Can I ask you something?'

'Of course.'

'Am I a good girl?'

The question takes Hannah by surprise. 'Of course you are. Why would you ask that?'

'Olivia's not, though, is she?'

Hannah sighs. They have already spoken about her sister and what happened at school, and she hoped that the conversation had been ended the day before. 'Olivia's got some problems at the moment. It's nothing for you to worry about.'

Rosie nods, processing the comment. 'Why do you think she's got problems?'

Hannah takes a deep breath. She doesn't have time for this, not today, not with everything else that is going on. Rosie is bright and naturally inquisitive, but Hannah hoped she wouldn't become like Olivia, always asking questions and needing to know more than is good for her.

'She's a teenager. It happens.'

She hopes the response will be enough, but apparently not. Rosie puts down her pencil and studies Hannah intently, a look that makes her feel uncomfortable. 'Why am I good and she's not?'

Hannah doesn't like the question; it feels loaded. 'What do you mean?'

'Well, what do I do that's good?'

Hannah smiles, relieved. What Rosie is asking is far more innocent than she first assumed. All her daughter wants is validation, she thinks, using this opportunity to have her own qualities praised, made more glorious against her wayward sister's.

'You do as you're told,' she says. 'You listen. You don't ask too many questions. Not until now, at least.' She smiles and taps the exercise book. 'Now get this finished up before you forget what you're doing.'

'Mum?'

'Is this another question?'

Rosie nods. 'A good one, though. When I'm finished, do you think I could have a bath, please?'

Hannah raises an eyebrow. It is usually all she can do to persuade Rosie to take a quick shower.

'I'd like to finish reading *A Dog's Life* in the bath.'

Hannah nods. 'Sounds like a good idea to me. There's some bubble bath in the cupboard above the sink.' She watches her daughter return her focus to her homework.

Hannah feels grateful for these peaceful moments, even more so when they occur amid the chaos that is taking place elsewhere. She thinks of Olivia upstairs in her bedroom, still immersed in her silence, and wonders whether she feels any remorse for the things she has done over this past week. Despite everything, Hannah doesn't believe she does. She doesn't know what it will take for her daughter to comprehend the scale of what she is doing to their family.

She wants to know what Michael said to Olivia this morning. She is sure that whatever it was, it hasn't gone down well. She wonders if he has mentioned what they've talked about: sending Olivia to a boot camp. When it was first suggested, Hannah almost laughed, it sounded so ridiculous. She has seen television programmes about these kinds of places, where troublesome teens are sent for rehabilitation, but it all sounds so foreign, the kind of thing once again that would apply to other families, never to hers. Yet here they are, considering it a very real possibility. Michael has pitched his justification, laid out his reasoning. It makes sense, as things always do with him. He is planning it with all their best intentions at heart.

Hannah is contemplating their uncertain future when she hears the doorbell ring. It is used so rarely – the postman, and the occasional salesperson – that the sound has become an alien one, and Hannah wonders for a moment whether she has been careless enough to leave her key in the door. She passes Rosie to get to the kitchen door and heads into the hallway. There is a silhouette on the other side of the glass, willowy and dark. Retrieving her keys from where they are kept, she unlocks the door.

There is a young woman standing on the doorstep, mixed race and pretty. She looks no older than her mid twenties and is wearing a short skirt with a pair of sheer tights and high-heeled ankle boots. Her dark hair is pulled back from her face, loose wisps hanging at her ears. Her eyes are lined with kohl, and oversized earrings hang from her lobes.

'Hannah?'

'Yes?' She wonders if she knows this girl; her name was spoken as though she is expected to recognise her.

'My name's Carly,' the young woman tells her. 'I need to talk to you about your husband.'

'What about my husband?'

Carly shifts her weight from one foot to the other, glancing past Hannah and into the house. Hannah steps defensively to one side, a subconscious attempt to block her view.

'I'd rather not speak to you out here. Could I come in?'

'No,' Hannah replies bluntly. She doesn't know what this girl wants or what trouble she intends to cause, but whatever her plans are, Hannah is about to stop them dead in their tracks. 'I don't know you. I don't know what you want, but Michael's not here.'

'I know that. That's why I've come. Please … I need to speak to you.'

Hannah feels her pulse start to quicken. She looks Carly up and down in a way she knows is judgemental, but she can't stop herself and she doesn't care. Whatever she wants to say to her, Hannah doesn't want to hear it.

'Mum.'

She turns sharply to see Rosie standing behind her, clutching her copy of *A Dog's Life*.

'Go upstairs,' Hannah tells her, and Rosie doesn't wait for a second instruction.

Hannah turns back to Carly. 'I'm busy, as you can see.' She pushes the door closed.

The girl puts a foot in the way, using her heel to try to stop it. 'You're making a mistake. You need to listen to me. Please, I really need to talk to you, and I don't think we should do it out here.'

Hannah pushes the door harder, not caring that she is cutting into the girl's ankle. At last Carly relents, and the door slams closed as she pulls away. Hannah falls against the hallway wall, breathing heavily, trying to fight back angry tears. A moment later, an envelope is pushed through the letter box. She waits for the girl to say something, to speak to her through the closed door, but she doesn't. She waits to hear her footsteps on the chippings of the driveway, listening to her leave, and even when she knows she is gone, she waits longer, not wanting to have to touch or look at what has been posted to her.

Yet she knows that she will. She cannot help herself.

She stoops and picks up the envelope. She takes it through to the kitchen and closes the door behind her. Sitting at the table, she opens it with shaking hands, knowing that whatever is inside, she needs to see it. She devours the words written there, words communicated purely for her consumption, swallowing them down as though she has not been fed for days. Each one makes her sick, poisoning her stomach with its intent. She has had enough, she is uncomfortably full, yet still she cannot stop reading.

By the end of the letter, her body is shaking. She goes to the cooker, lights one of the rings of the hob and stands with the letter held over it, trembling with the thought that a single lick of a flame could make all this go away. It would be so easy, she thinks.

And yet it isn't. She turns the dial of the cooker, killing the flame. With the letter still gripped in her trembling hand, she goes upstairs. The bathroom door is closed; she can hear water running as it fills the bath. She heads to her bedroom, and when she pushes the door open, she is greeted with a gasp. Rosie is kneeling on the carpet in front of her bedside table, its drawer pulled open.

'What are you doing in here?' Hannah feels blood rush to her temples and a sudden heat courses through her body, fuelling her with rage. 'Get out! Get out!'

Rosie rushes past her, slamming the door shut, and Hannah sits on the bed to cry silent, angry tears.

EIGHTEEN
OLIVIA

Olivia sits on her bed listening to the shouting coming from across the landing. It is only her mother's voice she hears, followed by the thundering of feet rushing past her room. She doesn't need to leave her bed to know what has happened, and she doesn't need to see her mother or Rosie to know that this is all her fault. She hopes Rosie isn't punished for being caught; she couldn't bear the guilt of being responsible for that. When she argued with her mother on Friday, Olivia meant every word, but she could never have imagined that things would go this far in such a short space of time.

As Olivia expects her to, Hannah appears at the bedroom door a while later. She has been crying, though she has made an effort to conceal the evidence. Olivia can't recall the last time she saw her mother cry, and she knows that she only ever does so in frustration. Something has happened. Whatever has managed to reduce her mother to tears, Olivia doesn't believe that finding Rosie in her bedroom is enough to have made her as angry as she is.

Hannah comes in and closes the door. Her mother is looking older, Olivia thinks; she has noticed it for a while now. She is only in her thirties but could easily pass for someone much older, someone worn down by life and all that it has thrown at her. She wonders whether Hannah has always been old, in the way that some people just seem to be. She can't be that many years older than Miss Johnson, yet the two of them couldn't be less alike. A permanent tiredness is etched in the skin around her mother's eyes and her shoulders are hunched as though in perpetual defeat. Olivia imagines that she should feel sorry for her, but she can't.

'Are you trying to make her like you now, is that it?' Hannah says, stepping closer to Olivia. Her voice is low and threatening. Of everything that has happened, Olivia suspects that this is the thing that will aggrieve her mother most. Involving her precious Rosie is the most heinous thing Olivia could possibly have done. 'You sent her looking for this, I suppose?'

She produces the diary, waving it in front of Olivia as though using it to torment her. In many ways, she is. Olivia knows that diary inside out, having read every page so many times. Her mother holds it in front of her before swiping it away again, giving Olivia no time to grab it from her grip.

'None of what is in here is any of your business,' Hannah tells her.

Olivia leans forward. 'Liar.'

The word is the first she has spoken to her mother in nearly a week, and she says it slowly, deliberately, unaware of the effect it will have. In recent days, Olivia has taken a perverse pleasure in watching her mother's frustrations grow, but now, looking at the reddened face and tightened fists, she realises she has no idea of just what her mother is capable of. There can be no satisfaction in seeing her so angry, seemingly on the edge of losing control. She will only be pushed so far before she snaps, and Olivia understands she has no comprehension of what might happen when she finally does.

'You really are poison, aren't you?' her mother says. 'I've always known it, but this week you've confirmed it for me.'

'Why did you tell us your mother was dead? Why doesn't she know you've got children?'

Hannah's face tells Olivia that she had no idea she has been to the care home and met with Eleanor. She can almost see the questions bouncing around her mother's brain, their shadows flitting across her eyes, crashing into one another in their desperation to be formed into words, because the diary alone gives no clue as to whether Eleanor is still alive. Her mother doesn't realise just how much Olivia knows. She might not know what her mother is capable of, but Hannah obviously underestimates Olivia too.

'Yeah, I've met her,' she says, giving her mother a forced smile. 'Nice little family reunion.'

'You have no idea what you've done, do you? You stupid, stupid little girl.'

Her mother can insult her all she wants; Olivia doesn't care. Hannah is a liar and she's been caught out. No matter what Olivia has done, her mother's sins far outweigh hers, and she must know it. Perhaps her anger is directed as much towards herself as towards Olivia. Surely she cannot fail to realise just how guilty she is.

'Are we that much of an embarrassment to you that you couldn't tell her we exist?'

Her mother's anger seems to fall from her, her face softens, and she sits at the foot of the bed, her body dropping onto the mattress in a defeated slump. She puts her elbows on her knees and her head in her hands and is silent for a moment, leaving Olivia wondering what's going on. Olivia recoils, pulling her feet to one side, not wanting them to make physical contact. Her mother is playing a game, she is sure of it, and she has no wish to take part in it.

'It's not about you,' Hannah says finally, raising her head and putting her hands in her lap. 'It's about her. Didn't you read this, then?'

Olivia has read the diary, countless times. She knows what is written about Eleanor, though none of it makes much sense. The woman she met was weak and vulnerable, with no traces of the domineering tyrant described in the entries penned by her own mother.

'My mother has a lot of problems,' Hannah begins to explain. 'She's very sick – she has been for a long time. Mentally, I mean.

She's been unstable for as long as I can remember. That's why she lives where she does now – it isn't safe for her to live alone any more.'

'But you used to look after her?'

'When I was younger, yes, but look, it's a lot more complicated than just what's in here. How did you find out she was still alive, anyway?'

'I heard you on the phone weeks ago. You said something about a visit, so I worked out that she was either in hospital or in some sort of home.'

Her mother smiles, but Olivia is unable to read the look. Though it may appear genuine, she cannot bring herself to believe there is any kindness in it. 'Too clever for your own good,' Hannah says. Her eyes scan the length of the bed, and Olivia reads the unspoken words that dangle silently from the sentence. *Not clever enough, obviously.*

'You know, whatever happened here on Saturday night …' Olivia waits for her mother to acknowledge her with a nod, 'it wasn't me.' She holds Hannah's gaze, trying to force her to believe the statement. She sees a flicker of something like doubt behind her eyes, though she isn't sure that it's enough. Her mother has made her mind up, but she is making a mistake. Olivia knows it wasn't her, so she therefore knows it must have been someone else. Someone else was in their home, someone who wants to unnerve her mother for some reason they don't yet know about. She is glad of it, relieved, but they still need to find out who that person is.

She glances at the diary in her mother's hand. There is something in it that needs explaining, something that has preyed on her mind repeatedly in the weeks since she found the notebook in her mother's room. How she didn't get caught she will never know, and now she feels so guilty for whatever reprimand Rosie will be forced to face.

'There's half a page missing,' she says. 'Like something's been ripped out. What was it?'

As quickly as it appeared, her mother's temporary softness evaporates and her anger returns, racing to her face like a flame. She looks at Olivia as though she hates her, which Olivia suspects she does. She has always suspected it. No matter what her mother tries to claim, Olivia has always felt herself treated differently. Rosie doesn't receive the contempt Olivia gets, and Olivia feels she never had the love her sister had. As a younger child, she would sometimes try to climb up onto her mother's lap, searching for nothing more than the warmth of an embrace. It was rarely given; she recalls times when her mother pushed her to one side and stood from where she had been sitting to address some job or other that she suddenly remembered she needed to do. Olivia would be left cold and rejected, wondering what she had done to make her mother so angry with her. It was never like that with Rosie. Olivia would watch the two of them play, Hannah chasing Rosie through the garden, and though their mother played with her as well, it always felt somehow different, as though the task of doing so was a duty, an undertaking she felt obliged to carry out.

Hannah holds the diary to her chest, protecting it as though fearful of what it might be capable of back in Olivia's hands. It doesn't matter, Olivia thinks; she has read and reread that half-page so many times that she can visualise it now, remembering almost word for word what is written there.

Dear Diary,
I'm sorry I haven't written in you
Something terrible has
it into words. I feel dirty.
keep going back over that night
happen, but I can't make any sense
time, I know that, but it feels
able to stop it. I can't tell anyone

Michael knows – he has been
would have done. I wish
this would have happened. I
was just the thought of what
I know different. I did the
supermarket when I was doing
seen it on the receipt. I am so
though I am carrying around
could make it go away, but
something beautiful come from
let him. There aren't many
to have found him, and I never
will learn to feel differently, I
hadn't already known, this would
me away from this life, give
to be saved.

The half-completed sentences have kept her awake at night, occupying her brain with how they might have read before the page was ripped in half and the second piece discarded. What had happened to her mother that made her feel dirty? What was it she couldn't tell anyone about? What was it that she felt she was carrying around with her? There are so many things Olivia wants to know, and though she realises she has pried into Hannah's secrets, she feels somehow that they are things she deserves to be aware of, things that affect her life as much as they do her mother's.

She recites the last few lines of the torn page, watching her mother's face as the realisation of just how many times Olivia has read the diary dawns upon her.

'What happened next?'

'This isn't a story, Olivia. This is my life. I'm entitled to my privacy.'

Olivia laughs, but there's no humour in the sound she makes; it is filled with ridicule and driven by scorn. She knows it and yet she doesn't care. Privacy is a topic her mother has no right to comment on, and she can think what she wants about Olivia. They have so little of their relationship now left to lose that it almost seems not to matter what happens from here on in. And yet it does. Despite everything, Olivia wants the truth.

'Oh, the irony.'

Her mother ignores the comment. 'There's a lot you don't understand about life. You think you're all grown up now, but you're still a little girl. You've proved that this past week.'

'Only because that's how you keep me. You won't let me do anything – you won't let me be a normal fifteen-year-old. If I'm still childish, it's because that's how you've made me.'

'All I've ever done is try to protect you.'

Here we go again, Olivia thinks. The guilt lecture. She has heard it so many times before, from her father as well as her mother, that she would be able to recite that back to her too.

'Protect me from what? From living? From having fun?'

'What's your idea of fun, Olivia? Getting drunk at parties? Wearing clothes that show off everything to everyone?'

Olivia rolls her eyes. 'You're being ridiculous. Is that all you think people my age get up to?'

Her mother's perception of being young has come from internet searches and Instagram posts, the false pictures painted by profiles such as Casey Cartwright's. Olivia knows plenty of the world's Casey Cartwrights – there are too many of them to count in her school year alone – but there are also many other types of teenagers, the kind Olivia would love to have the chance to be like. This is so typically judgemental of her mother, she thinks, and yet further evidence of how out of touch Hannah is with the real world that exists beyond the doors of their perfect home. There are things she wants to do, places she wants to see, but she will never get to do any of it while her mother seems so intent on ruling – and ruining – her life.

'You're young,' Hannah says, as though Olivia isn't already aware of the fact. 'There's a lot you've still got to learn. You think the world is this magical place where nothing bad ever happens, but you're wrong. I do understand, Liv. I was just like you once, remember.'

But Olivia knows this isn't the case. Her mother might have been fifteen once, but she was never anything like her; Olivia doesn't need to have seen her at that age to know it as fact. She was probably as old then as she is now, wanting nothing more than a nice kitchen and a husband to make dinner for, like some housewife from the type of 1950s advertisement they've studied in school. What sort of ambition is that, to be tied to the kitchen sink, a slave to domesticity? Olivia wants better for herself; something more than her mother has ever been able to imagine. She doesn't see why she should be condemned for dreaming.

'I'm not as stupid as you think I am. I know how dangerous the world is.'

Her mother laughs. 'You've no idea. The bad people far outweigh the good.'

Olivia wants to scream with frustration. She feels it building in her head, this pressure that bubbles and rises to the surface, swelling behind her temples. 'Well, you'd know all about that, wouldn't you?'

'What's that supposed to mean?'

There is silence between them for a moment while Olivia allows the comment time to settle. Her mother knows exactly what she means, and yet there are other things that make her bad, things she has never had to explain or justify to anyone.

'Well, what exactly did you do, Mother? This terrible thing that happened, this thing that made you feel so guilty you couldn't even bear to read it, so you had to rip the page out of your diary.

You love lecturing me, don't you, picking out all my mistakes, but what about you? What did you do that's so bad and so shameful?'

Her mother stares at her, her eyes emptied of all the anger that was there just moments ago, and when she speaks, Olivia feels the room shift beneath her, as though the floor has been pulled back and she is falling, with nothing to reach for to help break her landing.

'You stupid girl,' her mother says again. 'I was raped. Are you happy now?'

NINETEEN

HANNAH

There is an awful moment of silence in which neither of them knows what to say, and Hannah immediately regrets those three words that have fallen from her lips. She has kept this secret from her children – from everyone other than Michael – for years now, and she feels angry that she has been forced into speaking of it by her own daughter. Olivia can't leave things alone. She is dangerous and she will bring them all nothing but trouble. She has proved that by going to the care home and introducing herself to Eleanor. She had no right to, no right at all. She has no idea of the Pandora's box she is opening.

'When did it happen?'

Olivia thinks she is all grown up now, that she understands the world and the people in it, but this couldn't be further from the truth. Her continued questioning of Hannah about all this proves she is still a naïve little girl, still ignorant of the horrors that exist outside the four walls of this house. If she thinks that challenging her mother can make her talk to her about what happened when Hannah hasn't spoken a word of it in so many years, she is very much mistaken. Hannah doesn't even speak to Michael about it, not any more. They agreed a long time ago – after years of going over and over what happened that night and how she felt in its aftermath – that the best way to move on was to deal with it then, and to afterwards remove it from their history, though she never realised at the time just how difficult that would prove. Not difficult. Impossible.

'This has nothing to do with you, Olivia.'

Her face contorts. 'Why do you do this with everything? Any time I try to speak to you about anything, you change the subject or just blank it out. You can't stop me from wanting answers.'

'No, you're right,' Hannah tells her. 'But it doesn't mean I have to give them to you.'

Exasperated, Olivia moves to the wall and sits with her knees pulled up to her chest. Hannah thinks about leaving, but she knows it will not end here; Olivia will persist until she gets the answers she wants, or answers of some sort at least. The truth is that although Hannah pretends to Michael and to herself that she has moved what happened that night to the back of her brain, it is very much still at the forefront, still there when she closes her eyes at night. She sees that darkness and hears those noises in her dreams; if anything, being asleep is worse than being awake. During the day she can busy herself to keep at bay the thoughts she doesn't want to be haunted by, but at night there is nothing to distract her. The events of the past tower at the side of her bed, watching over her. They follow her into sleep and burn through any other dream that might try to take their place.

And now there is that letter, left with her as though its very existence means she must swallow down everything that is written there. She doesn't know who that girl is or what she's trying to do, but she won't let her try to hurt her like this. Hasn't her life been difficult and complicated enough without having to deal with all this now?

'What happened?'

Olivia's voice has changed; she sounds less aggressive than she did just moments ago. Hannah is still sitting on the edge of the bed, with Olivia now behind her, leaning against the bedroom wall.

She's glad her daughter can't see her face, or the shame she knows covers her like a veil each time she thinks about what happened that night.

'I know you hate me,' she says.

Behind her, she hears Olivia shift on the duvet. 'I don't hate you. You're my mum.'

Her daughter's words produce a charge of something unnameable that catches at her heart like an electric shock. Hannah recognises it for what it is, though she could never say it aloud. Guilt. Is this all it takes to earn a child's love, she wonders; simply the title of being mum? Is that how little it requires for someone to love you unconditionally, regardless of what you do in return? She wonders then if she should have loved her own mother more. She was there, wasn't she – controlling, manipulative, deceitful, but there, at least.

Hannah never met her father. He left when she was a baby, and as she grew older and saw her mother for what she really was, she realised exactly why he had gone. She just wished he had taken her with her, or at least stayed around to see her occasionally, though she forgave him for this, justifying his absence and his abandoning of her by reasoning that it was so much harder for a man to raise a child alone, and back in the eighties, at least, far less understood. In her mind, she has created an image of him as some sort of martyr, though on days when she is honest with herself, she realises that the depiction is a flawed one, and that in truth her mother was right when she told Hannah, repeatedly, that her father was a weak and cowardly man who ran away from his responsibilities.

'I've only ever tried to do what was best for you,' she tells Olivia. 'You think I'm controlling, but I just don't want you to make the same mistakes I did.'

Her daughter has no idea what controlling behaviour is really like. Hannah's mother was an expert in manipulation, feigning for years an illness Hannah now questions ever existed at all. Eleanor's

ME – or her claims to it, at least – dominated their lives. From an early age, Hannah was responsible for the cooking, the cleaning and the washing, her mother simply not up to the physical demands that looking after a home and raising a child required. Eleanor would go to Hannah's school occasionally and when it was expected – annual parents' evenings and end-of-summer sports days – but eventually even those visits faded out, and Hannah would be the only child in the school show with no one in the audience to watch her, the one who walked home alone in the dark, the original latch-key kid.

By the time she was at secondary school, her mother's condition, both physical and mental, had deteriorated at a speed for which Hannah was unprepared. Eleanor became angrier and more demanding, going as far as to blame Hannah for the state she was now in, claiming that childbirth had ruined her life. By now, she never left the house, her entire existence confined within the four walls of the box that was their home, and Hannah's only trips into the outside world involved either school or the weekly food shop. She started to believe that her mother might have been right, and that it would have been better for them both had she never been born.

'When you went to that party ...' Hannah starts, but her sentence fades into silence as the past returns to stand beside her, looming over her and casting her into its shadow. Her thoughts last Friday were filled with the darkest images, things she didn't want to imagine but her mind wouldn't let her unsee. She wouldn't want anyone to go through what she had, and the thought of it happening to her own daughter filled her with horror. The letter reads itself out again in her head, though she tries to drown it out with the noise of other thoughts. There was something about that girl's face that was so recognisable, though she was sure she had never seen her before.

'I went to a party too,' she confesses, remembering how she managed to sneak from the house when her mother was asleep.

'I was just like you, Olivia, although I know you probably think we've never had anything in common. I always wanted more than I had; I was always fantasising about some other, better life. I used to look at other girls and think about how much more exciting their lives were than mine. I got dressed up, too dressed up, and I went out, even though I'd been told not to.'

'What do you mean "too dressed up"?'

'Well, not dressed enough, really. Showing too much, like the other girls did.'

'And that night was when …'

Hannah nods. 'I was on my way home. I'd had too much to drink and I decided to take a shortcut through the park. I was only three streets from home. I was hit over the back of the head with something. It knocked me out for a while, but it wasn't for long enough.'

She stops; she can't talk about this any more. What happened that night is as blurred now as it was then, her senses impaired by the alcohol she had consumed and the injury she sustained. She remembers shadows, noises, her mind slipping in and out of consciousness as her body endured what she was powerless to stop. He was behind her, on top of her, and it was all over so quickly. Yet it seemed it would never end, and in so many ways it hasn't.

She stands from the bed. 'I'll bring you up a cup of tea and something to eat,' she says, as though the conversation they have just had never happened.

'I'm sorry.'

She turns at the words, not believing that they have come from Olivia's mouth. Her daughter is never sorry for anything, not even when she should be. She rarely shows anyone an ounce of empathy, usually too busy caught up in feeling sorry for herself or thinking about her own needs.

'I'm sorry that happened to you,' Olivia says, and for a moment she sounds as though she means it, but when she speaks again, the sentiment is snatched away. 'But it doesn't justify how you treat me.'

Hannah studies her daughter's face: the defiance in her jawline; the rage that rests behind her tired eyes. She isn't sorry at all, she thinks; she is still only sorry for herself, still consumed with her own selfish desires.

'How old were you?'

She holds Olivia's stare, knowing that this moment is likely to change everything. She should hold this information back, keep it stored where it has been buried for so long. There are repercussions, and yet she realises that everything is falling around their ears already. Olivia won't give up until she gets what she wants. If what she really wants is the truth, Hannah is now prepared to offer it to her.

'I was seventeen.'

She watches as Olivia does the mental maths, her face changing instantly. In a moment – one so brief yet so life-shattering – she seems to realise that in pushing for the truth, she is opening a nightmare. Hannah knows she should feel sympathy for her, and yet she can't. Olivia has asked for this, always prying into things that don't concern her; always wanting more than she has, needing to know more than her young brain can handle. Perhaps she deserves to know, so she will realise just how much her parents have given her. Hannah and Michael have done everything they can to give Olivia the kind of life Hannah herself would have given anything for, and yet nothing has ever been good enough for her. She has taken and taken, always pushing and pushing, never satisfied with what she has.

Olivia opens her mouth to say something, but nothing comes out. She has worked it out, or is beginning to, at least. She knows that this act of violence is where she began. Her already pale face whitens further, and she shakes her head, looking at Hannah as though her presence alone has managed to burn her.

'Is that when I was …?' But she can't finish the sentence, can't bring herself to find the words. She is unable to believe that she was conceived in such a way. Despite all the times she has hated her parents, she doesn't want to have to face the fact that her father isn't her father at all.

Hannah nods, the gesture all she can offer her.

Olivia gulps down a sob, fighting herself from showing tears. 'This is why you hate me, isn't it? This is why you've always loved Rosie so much more than you love me, and why sometimes you can't even bring yourself to look at me. Everything makes sense now. You shouldn't have gone through with the pregnancy. I would have been better off dead.'

Hannah has felt so often in recent times that she doesn't know who her own daughter is, but she has always known why this is; deep down, she has always understood the reason why she remains a stranger to her. She isn't like them. She never could be. There has always been some darkness in her, something that longs to cause chaos and wreak destruction. Hannah isn't responsible for any of it. It is in Olivia, this sickness; it is a part of him, the man who attacked her.

'Your father and I are sending you away,' she says flatly, her voice numbed of any kind of emotion. 'I think he's already discussed it with you.'

Olivia shakes her head. 'You can't do this,' she objects. 'My exams are starting in a few weeks – you can't just send me away now.'

'We are your parents,' Hannah says, as though Olivia needs any reminding of the fact. 'It is our responsibility to do what's best for you, and at the moment you're a danger to yourself. Where does this stop, Olivia? You seem intent on doing everything you can to ruin things for yourself and for this family. We have a responsibility to protect Rosie as well.'

'Separating us isn't protecting her!' Olivia shouts.

'And turning out like you … would that be better? I have to think of both of you, Olivia, and this is what's best for everyone.'

'Best for you, you mean. Send me away before anyone finds out what a psychopath you are!'

Hannah's hand swings forward, her palm held open. But it doesn't make contact with Olivia's face as her daughter so obviously expects it to. Instead, it stops just centimetres from her, held there with the threat of what might have happened. She won't hit her; she won't ever hit her. This is what Olivia wants, what she has always wanted, just so that Hannah will appear the troubled one and Olivia can prove that she is right. She cannot allow herself to lose control. Once that happens, she knows she will have lost, and Michael will never forgive her.

TWENTY

OLIVIA

Olivia lies in bed, her eyes open, staring into the darkness that surrounds her. Even if there was any chance of her being able to find sleep, she knows it would be shattered by nightmares, by all the things she doesn't want to have to think about but can't prevent from gathering like the imagined monsters of her childhood, this time real. The monsters are with her now, standing by her bedside. They take different forms, each faceless, and she doesn't want to have to believe that one of them is her father. Her real father.

She has never seen her mother as she saw her this evening; she is usually so composed and in control, as though nothing ever makes her uneasy or is capable of sending her perfect world off balance. Just a few weeks earlier, Olivia might have believed that witnessing her mother so vulnerable would have been something she would relish, but she has seen a different side to her over this past week – yet another version of the woman who seems to wear so many faces – and she can take no pleasure in it, not when it has been created by something so unspeakable.

She wonders why Hannah kept her. So much makes sense to her now – the coldness, the distance, the lack of love her mother has so often showed her. It makes sense to her now why Rosie has always been the child favoured by both her mother and her father, and yet it occurs to her too that none of this was her fault. She didn't ask to be brought into this world. Her mother could have got rid of her if she had wanted to, and perhaps that would have been better for them all. They have made her an outsider, and now she doesn't know how to be anything else.

She doesn't want to believe that any of what her mother has said is true, least of all that she was conceived in such a way and that her father isn't her father at all. This is the part that is hardest for Olivia, because if Michael isn't her father then some stranger is, some stranger capable of the worst kind of violence, a kind that until now she has only heard about and has never had to accept exists in her own world. She thinks of her mother as she might have been at seventeen, not much older than Olivia herself is now. She does understand her mother's behaviour, why she is so overprotective towards her, though she would never admit as much. She understands why Hannah doesn't want her to go to parties and be around people who might turn out to be the wrong sort, but at the same time she can't keep her wrapped in cotton wool forever. What happened to her mother is now responsible for ruining Olivia's life too, and like so much else, it just doesn't seem fair that she is being made to suffer for the actions of someone else, someone she has never even met and someone who, regardless of genetics, is nothing to do with her in any way.

Olivia cannot get past the thought of just how much she looks like Michael. Where Rosie has always been like their mother, long-limbed and slim, Olivia is shorter and naturally heavier, with the same hair colouring as her father, a kind of mousy brown that in him is now succumbing to the early signs of grey, where he hasn't started balding. She looks like him around the eyes. They have the same-shaped face. But it is easy to see what you expect to see, she thinks, particularly when you have no reason to be looking for anything other.

Her mother will try to use what happened to her years ago as justification for everything she does now, and though Olivia knows that what happened is appalling, it doesn't make right what Hannah has done or how she behaves. She assumes it was Eleanor who told Hannah not to go to that party, and that after what happened, she now looks back at that night and feels she should have listened. Her own mother may have been right on one occasion, but that doesn't mean Hannah is right about everything now.

The way she spoke about what happened to her isn't normal, Olivia feels certain of that. It sounded almost as though she was blaming herself, as though by not listening, she deserved what was coming to her. The way she talked about what she wore – some comment about not being dressed enough – doesn't seem right to Olivia either. She knows she has a lot to learn and that in many ways she is still so young, despite no longer wanting to be. But her mother underestimates her. She has a greater understanding of things than Hannah gives her credit for, and one thing she feels certain of is that an attack such as the one her mother endured is never justified, irrespective of what she might or might not have been wearing.

Olivia thinks a lot about injustice and how much of it exists around her, both in her own world and in the wider one being experienced by everybody else. The time spent in this room, prone in her bed, has given her plenty of time to think, whether she wants to or not. As far as she can tell, it is the quiet people who suffer, the ones who fade into the background, willingly or otherwise, and allow themselves to be overshadowed by larger, louder characters. She loves to people-watch, though she doesn't get to do it often, and has witnessed this type of injustice plenty of times at school. She has seen the quiet ones in her class disappear behind the loud-mouths and the look-at-mes, gradually fading until they become invisible, until even the best teachers stop seeing them. She can identify these victims of injustice because she is one of them. For too long she has allowed herself to fade, but not any more. People are noticing her now.

She is due to start her GCSE exams in little over three weeks' time. She has worked hard for them – not as hard as she might have done under different circumstances, but she has done her best and couldn't have given it any more than she has – but now she wonders whether the effort she has put in has all been for nothing. If she were to sail through with a bunch of A* grades, what use would they be to her anyway? Where would they take her?

The thought brings everything flooding back, the threat that her father and now her mother have made hitting her with a force that feels almost physical. She wondered at first whether her father was trying to scare her, his words delivered in that hushed tone he only uses to let her know that she is in the worst kind of trouble, but now – now that the threat has been echoed by her mother – she realises that they mean it, and perhaps she has pushed them too far this time. She considers what it might mean for her, as well as for Rosie, but she knows it isn't as straightforward as her brain is trying to make it. Her parents have thought this through in meticulous detail; they will have considered every possible scenario and each potential outcome. They won't leave anything to chance; in Olivia's experience, they rarely do. While her mind has tried to reassure her that maybe this will all be for the best in the end, she cannot bring herself to believe that that is true. For the first time in her life, she wants to stay exactly where she is. She needs to be here.

Above everything else that scares her, brings tears to her tired eyes, it is being separated from Rosie that fills her with the greatest fear. Despite all the times her sister has driven her to distraction, and all the occasions Olivia has felt herself belittled by her, jealous of the relationship Rosie has with their mother, she knows that theirs is her best friendship, and she doesn't want to be torn from it. She feels sorry for what she did now, sorry that she behaved in that way at school, and sorry that those videos of her are now all over the internet, but she still doesn't believe this is all her fault, not really, because if her parents hadn't treated her the way they did, then none of this would have happened. She doesn't deserve to be punished for it, and Rosie shouldn't be made to suffer.

She is filled with remorse that Rosie might have to deal with the consequences of her actions. People at Rosie's primary school will be aware of what happened; they will remember Olivia from her time there and they will know what she has done. She doesn't want Rosie to be ridiculed or embarrassed by what is now displayed of her across the internet, but she believes now more than ever that her sister understands things better than she has ever given her credit for. They need each other. Perhaps this once, Olivia needs Rosie more than Rosie needs her.

Her parents might have their plans, she thinks, but she is capable of making her own. If she doesn't act quickly, it will be too late, and her life will be changed beyond recognition, perhaps irreversibly so. She must do something, and she has to do it soon, and whether either of them likes it or not, she is going to need Rosie's help.

TWENTY-ONE

HANNAH

Being forced into a confession by her fifteen-year-old daughter was never the way in which Hannah envisaged her secret might one day be released into the world. As soon as the words left her mouth, she regretted them, though she is sure Olivia wouldn't have stopped until she had got to the truth one way or another. She needs to speak to her again now, to get her to promise that she will keep the secret to herself, but just how much this can be relied upon, she can't be sure. She has no confidence left in her daughter, and Michael doesn't deserve to have his world ripped from beneath him. He has done everything for Olivia, bringing her up as his own and treating her no differently to Rosie. It is Hannah who is guilty of that, though she has never been able to do anything about it. Perhaps she hasn't tried hard enough, but it has been difficult when sometimes merely looking at her daughter takes her back to that place and that night.

Now all she can do is pray that Olivia does the right thing and doesn't tell Michael what she knows. If he finds out, it will break him.

She isn't expecting the knock at the door that comes at around 3.40 p.m. Her thoughts have been filled with Olivia and with that letter that was shoved her way by a stranger, and she is snapped from them with a force that feels violent. She feels tired and fraught and the last thing she needs is to speak to any outsiders, but when she peers through the living room window at the people on the doorstep, she recognises Olivia's head of year, Mr Lewis. She doesn't know the young woman standing beside him.

She pushes her hair behind her ears and wipes a careful finger under each eye, trying to hide any evidence of her exhaustion.

'Mrs Walters,' Mr Lewis says, extending his hand in greeting. 'I hope we're not interrupting anything. This is Miss Johnson, Olivia's English teacher.'

Hannah smiles, but it is not reciprocated. She takes an immediate dislike to this woman; she doesn't know why, but there is something about the way the woman glances furtively around her, as though searching for something, that makes her feel uneasy. 'House visits are unusual,' she says, trying to make the comment sound as casual as possible.

'We know you're busy,' Mr Lewis said. 'We thought we'd save you the bother of having to come back to us.' He smiles and gestures to the hallway. 'Okay if we come in? We won't keep you long.'

Hannah pauses before stepping aside and ushering them into the house. She notices the way Miss Johnson glances up the staircase. 'Everything okay?' she asks, but the woman doesn't even have the decency to appear embarrassed by her obvious nosiness.

Miss Johnson and Mr Lewis follow Hannah into the kitchen, where she gestures for them to take a seat. 'What can I do for you?'

'Is Olivia home?' Miss Johnson asks.

'No. I know it's probably wrong, what with her being on suspension and everything, but she's gone out with her father and her sister. What is it they say – children deserve your love the most when they deserve it the least? Something like that, anyway. We thought it might do her some good to spend some time with Rosie. We're hoping she'll have a calming effect on her.'

'Where have they gone?'

'The beach. It's a lovely day; seemed sensible to make the most of it.'

'A three-month heatwave is on the cards, so I've heard,' Mr Lewis says conversationally. 'Save a bit of money on a holiday abroad, won't it?'

Miss Johnson flashes him a look that isn't missed by Hannah. Whatever they are here for, the woman clearly wants to omit the small talk and get straight to the matter in hand.

'We have some new concerns about Olivia, I'm afraid, Mrs Walters,' Mr Lewis says, as though reminding himself why they're there. 'Miss Johnson has brought a couple of things to our attention.'

Hannah looks at her, waiting for her to explain. 'Shall I make tea?' she suggests when Miss Johnson says nothing.

Mr Lewis accepts the offer, so Hannah sets about filling the kettle and taking mugs from the cupboard. She glances at the two teachers sitting at the table and catches a look passed between them. Their presence doesn't bode well for any of them. If Michael were here now, how would he deal with this?

'There was an incident during Olivia's English lesson on Monday,' Miss Johnson says, as Hannah goes to the fridge to take out the milk. 'One of the boys made a derogatory comment about her, suggesting she might be able to explain the behaviour of Curley's wife in the book we're studying.'

Hannah pours water from the kettle into each of the three mugs before adding milk. 'What sort of comment?'

'Well, the character is accused of being a—'

'What did he say, Miss Johnson?' Hannah says, her back still turned. 'What was the comment?'

'We were talking about why the character behaves the way she does, and one of the boys said, "Ask Olivia, she'll be able to explain it."'

Hannah carries the three mugs over to the table and puts them down before sitting opposite the teachers. 'That doesn't tell me a lot. What's he suggesting, that Olivia is bright and might be able to answer the question better than anyone else?' She smiles thinly. 'Sounds like a compliment to me.'

Miss Johnson returns the smile, its corners hard-edged. 'I wish that were the case, Mrs Walters, but unfortunately, I think there was more to it than that. The character in the book is considered … promiscuous, shall we say. The boy in question was making the suggestion that Olivia might behave in the same way. Olivia looked very embarrassed by the incident.'

The party, Hannah thinks. Something happened at that party last Friday night, something the whole school no doubt knew about by Monday morning. Whatever it was, Olivia obviously didn't learn from it, not if Wednesday was anything to go by. Just what the hell else has she been up to?

Mr Lewis picks up his mug and takes a sip of tea. 'One of the girls made a comment then, something Miss Johnson only picked up on as possibly relevant after Wednesday's incident.'

Hannah looks at Miss Johnson expectantly. 'And that was?'

'She said the character behaves that way for attention.'

She raises her arms. She knows she is being patronising, but she cannot help herself, not when this is such a waste of everyone's time. 'An accurate analysis, don't you think? I'd say you've done an excellent job, Miss Johnson; it sounds as though your class is well prepped for the exam.'

Miss Johnson purses her lips, making no effort to hide her annoyance. 'The girl was looking at Olivia when she made this comment. I think she was talking about Olivia rather than the character in the book. What happened on Wednesday, don't you think it was maybe a cry for attention?'

'She certainly got plenty of that,' Hannah says, not bothering to try to keep the sarcasm from her voice. 'I'm sorry, Miss Johnson, but I'm not sure what you're trying to get at here. Olivia is fifteen years old. It's not the easiest age, you'll know that. Her behaviour has changed recently, but it hasn't been significantly different to that of any other teenager. She's hit a rebellious phase, that's all. They all do it.'

'Olivia has lost a lot of weight. Quite a dramatic amount in such a short time.'

Hannah sighs. 'I discussed this with Mrs Parker. Lots of girls Olivia's age are conscious of the way they look; there isn't anything unusual there either. Now, I appreciate your concern for my daughter's well-being, but this really is a waste of everyone's time. What happened this week has obviously been difficult for the whole family, as I'm sure you'll appreciate, but it won't happen again, I can assure you of that. Does Mrs Parker know you're here?'

The furtive look that passes between the two teachers answers Hannah's question for her. She feels control slip back into her hands with the knowledge that if the head was to find out about this home visit, both Mr Lewis and Miss Johnson would find themselves in trouble for it.

'Thought not. I must make a note to let her know first thing in the morning.'

Ignoring Hannah's threat, Miss Johnson rifles through her bag, then slaps a photocopied A4 piece of paper on the table between them. 'Exam practice,' she says. 'The students had to pick a title and spend forty minutes writing a story. Olivia chose the title "The Visitor" and wrote this. Go ahead,' she adds, pushing the paper nearer to Hannah.

Hannah takes it, feeling anticipation peak in the pit of her stomach. Everything Olivia has done recently seems designed to cause maximum mayhem, and she doubts this will be any different.

The Visitor

There was once a girl who lived in an ordinary house, on an ordinary street. Her world looked normal, much like anyone else's, but normal can be deceiving and can wear a misleading costume. Like everyone else her age, she went to school, but this was where the similarities ended. No one at school liked her; they thought she was strange. She *was* strange: she dressed differently; her hair was different; she didn't seem to fit in anywhere and wouldn't if she tried.

One Friday evening, this girl went to a party. She had never been to a party before and it was exciting and loud and scary in all the best sort of ways. She didn't know what to do or how to behave, so she had a drink to calm her nerves. It tasted sweet and horrible, but she drank a bit more when it started to make her feel better. She danced. People laughed at her, but she didn't care; this was the best night of her life so far and it didn't matter what they said about her at school on Monday.

A boy asked her to go upstairs with him, so she did. They kissed. Then he asked her to do something to him, something she'd never done before. She wasn't really sure about it, but she knew that some of the other girls in her year had done it and she thought that she might like it if she tried it once. She didn't, but it didn't seem to matter at the time. She was starting to live.

Hannah stops reading, though she is only midway through the story. She doesn't want to read any more, but she knows she must reach the end. Her stupid, reckless daughter, she thinks – is that what her idea of living is? Giving blow jobs to strange boys in strangers' houses? She despairs of what Olivia has become, not knowing what she is going to do with her. She feels her face flush with the shame of it all, knowing that both Mr Lewis and Miss Johnson are watching her, waiting for a reaction to what she has read. She feels sick at the thought of how Michael will react to this, not wanting him to know what has become of their daughter. Perhaps now he might start to accept that there are things about Olivia, these ways she has, that are beyond their control.

When she glances up, the English teacher's eyes are focused on her, accusing her with a silent stare. Hannah feels like reaching across the table to slap her.

By Monday, the whole school knew what she had done. She heard them talking in the corridors and whispering behind her back in assembly, calling her names she'd only ever heard used about other people before. She knows she should care more, but she can't, because whether rightly or wrongly, people are starting to notice her. She needs someone to notice her.

She goes to the beach and stands on the pier, breathing in the cold air of the sea. It feels nice on her lungs, fresh and new. She has never been to the seaside before; she didn't know that it was there all along, that close to her home. She watches the birds as they circle in the sky overhead and she thinks about what it might mean to be able to fly, to just spread her wings and take off from the ground, leaving her life behind her and soaring to a new one, wherever it might be.

Because behind the doors of this girl's normal home and the appearance of her normal life, things happen to her that she realises now are anything but normal. She isn't allowed outside, not unless it's in the garden or to school, where her mother still walks her every day as though she is still seven years old. She isn't allowed friends or contact with the outside world. She can watch television sometimes, but only when and what her parents decide she is allowed. She can read, but every book that comes into the house from school must be checked over by one of her parents first. There are locks on the windows to stop her trying to escape, and if she breaks her parents' rules, there are handcuffs on the bed that are fastened around her ankles and – when they've decided she's been really bad – sometimes around her wrists.

She doesn't believe in God, but the girl prays that a visitor will come one day, someone who will knock at the door unexpectedly and find what no one else has seen, things that she can't say aloud to anyone because she is scared and she doesn't want to lose her sister. Perhaps a teacher will come, she thinks, someone she can trust and can rely on to help her and her sister escape their prison. Please, she thinks, send help. Come quickly.

Hannah sighs and looks up from the page. 'It's well written, isn't it? What would it get in the exam?'

She doesn't like the way Miss Johnson is looking at her. Beside her, Mr Lewis is staring at his hands, his face flushed pink, too embarrassed to make eye contact with either of them.

'It's a strange interpretation of the title,' she adds, when neither teacher answers her question. 'My daughter is certainly imaginative.'

'Is there nothing you find worrying in this?' Miss Johnson asks.

'Plenty,' Hannah admits, 'but you know how dramatic teenagers can be.' She stops to gauge the teachers' reactions. 'You're not suggesting that any of this is based on reality, are you?' she says, passing the story back to Miss Johnson. 'Please,' she adds, gesturing to the door. 'Go ahead … be my guest. Take a look around if you like.'

The two teachers glance at one another, and Hannah sees the slight shake of the head that Mr Lewis offers Miss Johnson, as though warning her that this charade has gone far enough.

'I can't tell you how insulting this is,' she says. 'My husband and I are beside ourselves with worry about Olivia's behaviour, and now you come into my home and accuse me of … what, exactly? Imprisoning my own daughter?'

For the first time, even Miss Johnson has the good grace to blush. Beside her, Mr Lewis looks as though he can't wait to be away from this room and this house. Hannah is surprised he has allowed himself to be dragged here on this fool's errand; it is obvious whose idea it was to come here this afternoon.

'Let's call him,' she says, standing and going to the far end of the kitchen to retrieve her mobile from the windowsill. 'My husband,' she adds, pulling the charger from the phone. 'I'll call him for you.'

She finds Michael's number and puts the call on loudspeaker, allowing them all to hear the ringing and wait for an answer. It goes through to answerphone, and she cuts the call at the sound of his voice introducing himself. 'He's probably left his phone in the car,' she says, putting the mobile into her pocket. 'You're welcome to wait for him to call back, if you like.'

'That won't be necessary,' Mr Lewis says, standing. 'Thank you for your time, Mrs Walters,' he adds, though his colleague gets up without speaking, not hiding the look of contempt she offers Hannah. 'I'm sure you'll understand our need to follow this up.'

Hannah nods. 'Of course. I'm sure you'll do the right thing and let Mrs Parker know all about it tomorrow. Probably best to hear it from you first before I call her. I'll be speaking to Olivia about it as well. There's no one more worried about her behaviour at the moment than I am.'

They leave without further comment, and Hannah closes the front door too heavily behind them, her heart pounding at the exchange that's just taken place. She stands with her back to the door for a moment, feeling her body shaking, desperately trying to compose herself.

After a minute, she goes upstairs and into Olivia's room. Her daughter is lying in bed, her mouth still stuffed with a rolled-up pair of socks, the first thing that came to hand when Hannah heard the knocking at the front door. Her face is red with frustration and wet with tears; there are welts and blood on her wrists where she has fought to free herself of her restraints.

Ignoring the muffled cries that Olivia desperately tries to expel, Hannah takes her mobile from her pocket and calls Michael's number. She waits again for it to ring through to the voicemail service, this time listening to his message and speaking after the beep.

'Her teachers have just been here. What we've talked about, about sending Olivia away. We need to do it. We need to do it soon.'

TWENTY-TWO

OLIVIA

Olivia doesn't know where her mother is, whether she's at home or has gone out somewhere, though she doubts she will have gone anywhere with her still here in the house. She has stopped struggling against her restraints, having realised that her efforts are futile and are only serving to heighten the pain that fills her arms. She is used to the cuffs that lock her ankles to the bed frame; her parents use these often, and quite regularly at night. She has worn trousers and leggings in warm weather to conceal the marks they have sometimes left, and she has become accustomed to finding excuses that have removed her from having to take part in PE lessons. Olivia has tried to escape before, once, but her parents made sure she hasn't been able to do it again. They don't usually restrain her completely, but when her mother heard the door, she must have looked out from the front window and seen who was there. She told Olivia to keep her mouth shut, though she wasn't given the chance to do anything but that.

Olivia cried when she heard Miss Johnson's voice at the foot of the stairs. She had read her story; she knew what was going on. She fought desperately to make herself heard, but the more she tried to scream, the more her mouth dried up around the socks her mother had put there, and the more her throat burned with the effort of trying to make herself heard. Her mother has never gone this far. She was panicking, surely realising that she and Michael can't keep this up forever. It is the only thing that has kept Olivia going. For a while – for too long – she believed that this *would* be forever. Now she understands that sooner or later, she will escape this hell they call a home.

She wishes now that she had spoken to someone ages ago, when she first realised that the way her family lives isn't the way everyone else's does. Once she started at secondary school, the situation started to look a little different, though she still put most things down to the fact that she knew she was a little odd, a little out of touch with the cooler, more streetwise kids. By the end of year nine, she understood that it wasn't just this; that there was far more to the situation than simply her own detachment. Yes, she was different, but her parents had made her so, keeping her trapped in this house like a prisoner, segregated from the outside world and blind to everything it might have to offer.

She has missed out on birthday parties, school trips, days out at the seaside, all the things she realises now make up part of a normal childhood. They have been on holiday, twice, but Olivia suspects that these two isolated occurrences were more about presenting an appearance of normality to the outside world than about actually spending time together as a family doing normal family things. The last holiday was six years ago, when she was too young and too naïve to see what was going on. She wonders if either of her parents noticed the point at which it no longer became safe for them to play out the pretence in public.

They want to send her away because they know they are beginning to come undone. Her parents think she is stupid, but Olivia understands far more than they give her credit for. They think that by sending her to one of these so-called boot camps, they will make anything Olivia might claim there incredible, because who will believe the words of a girl who is so wayward and out of control that her own parents have relinquished responsibility for her and admitted defeat? They think no one will believe her when she tells them about what happens here; that she is a story-teller, a fantasist, a dangerous child who wishes to wreak destruction upon her family's reputation.

When she stood on that pier, looking at the sea, earlier in the week, she felt something stir in her, some longing that her mother has described as a restlessness. Hannah has made her feel as though she is ungrateful, undeserving of all that her parents do for her, yet all they have done is keep her trapped. She wants to feel sand between her toes. She wants to breathe in cold mountain air. She wants to swim with fish in a bottomless ocean. She wants to walk through a shopping centre in the same way anyone else might, an act apparently so mundane and everyday to everyone else, yet so alien to her.

Olivia thought that Rosie had yet to realise how different their lives are from those of the other kids at their schools, though their conversation on Wednesday night suggests she sees and understands more than she has been letting on. She is so much more aware than Olivia was at her age, and now Olivia realises just how much she has underestimated her younger sister.

It has been the fear of being separated from Rosie that has kept Olivia from confiding in anyone from the outside world. Nearly two and a half years ago, when she first questioned her parents about the way they lived, they warned her that if she was ever to tell anyone what went on in the house, she and Rosie would be separated and would never see each other again. Though Rosie is able to wind Olivia up more than anyone else in this world, Olivia loves her more than she loves anyone. She is all the family she has.

In more recent times, with Olivia growing increasingly questioning and challenging of her parents' behaviour, they told her that no one would believe what she said. Who would trust the stories of a girl known to be a troublemaker? The break-in at the house last Saturday night, the faked phone call from Rosie's school ... these are all now ammunition to their claims that Olivia is out of control. They have set her up in the worst of ways, the cruellest and most twisted they could have possibly imagined. But why wouldn't they? Cruel and twisted is what her parents are.

Olivia begins to cry again, overcome with the hopelessness of her situation. She wanted to protect Rosie, to get them both out of this house unharmed, but now she fears that will never happen. Miss Johnson and Mr Lewis left here thinking everything is normal, presumably with the notion that she is a troubled, attention-seeking drama queen. If they don't believe her, she fears that no one will. There is no one else who will come to her rescue.

She hears a noise, and Rosie's face appears around the door.

'Get out,' Olivia hisses. If their mother finds her in here, Rosie will end up chained to her bed too, and then between them they really won't be able to do a thing to get themselves out of this place. Olivia knows that her parents do the same to Rosie sometimes, punishing her for an escape she has never yet tried to make, though she knows that it happens to her sister far more infrequently than it does to her.

Ignoring Olivia's instruction, Rosie pushes open the bedroom door softly and tiptoes into the room, trying to avoid the creaky floorboards under the middle of the carpet. 'Are you okay?' she whispers.

'I'm fine,' Olivia lies, 'but you won't be if she catches you in here.'

'Something weird is going on.'

No shit, Olivia thinks, but she tries not to let Rosie see how frustrated she's becoming. She doesn't want her sister to be scared, though there is plenty to fear all around them.

Rosie sits on the bed and holds her phone out so that Olivia can see its screen. It has always seemed strange to Olivia that her parents permit them to have mobile phones, though internet access is restricted and their use is monitored by their father. It has occurred to her that in some ways it is just another form of torture inflicted upon them, allowing them occasional glimpses of a world that they have never truly been allowed to be a part of. Sometimes, when she has been permitted to access the internet to complete her homework, she has searched for images of beaches and mountains, losing herself to the thought of being somewhere as far away from this place as possible. Every picture has made her sadder; every fantasy of freedom has made her more determined to escape. She thought those places were a world away, yet she knows now that freedom is just the other side of the front door.

Their father has always checked their phones daily, going through their internet history to see what they have looked at when they were allowed access. They are only permitted to have them when their parents have agreed it, and if they want to look at something specific, they must ask permission first. Olivia was careful to delete her call history after phoning around the local care homes, knowing that either her mother or father would see it and find out what she had been doing. She wouldn't usually dare look at anything that hadn't been passed by one of them first; it isn't worth the punishment that such a crime would be met with. Though she hates being around them, whole weekends of isolation while chained to her bed are far worse, and there is no doubt that if either Rosie or she was to break the rules, they would get found out. They always seem to get found out.

She looks at the screen that Rosie is holding out in front of her. It is a news report with the headline *Body on Beach Identified*.

'Have you heard about this?'

'How have you got onto that?'

'Homework. It came up on the home page. Have you seen it?'

'Funnily enough, no. I don't get out much these days, I don't know if you'd noticed.'

'Everyone at school has been talking about it,' Rosie says, ignoring her sister's sarcasm. 'A woman was found this morning – her body was washed up on the beach. It looked like she'd drowned at first, but people are saying now that she was murdered. Look.'

Rosie scrolls the page and a photograph of the woman appears on the screen. She is young, pretty, but there is something sad behind her eyes, something silently screaming at the camera or whoever is behind it. And then Olivia realises who she is looking at. The woman with the young boy who was here in their street on Monday. The woman who asked her for the time.

'Why are you showing me this?' she asks, hoping her voice doesn't betray her. She doesn't want to make Rosie more afraid than she might already be.

'Because she was here,' Rosie says, glancing at the open bedroom door, and Olivia tastes sickness in her mouth, sour and sharp. 'Yesterday. She was here, on the doorstep. Mum was talking to her and she got really weird with me when she saw me in the hall behind them, like she couldn't wait to get rid of me.'

Olivia looks at the woman's face again. Prior to Monday afternoon, she had never seen her before, and she doesn't know why her mother might have been speaking to her, or why any of this might be relevant to them. 'It couldn't have been the same woman.'

'It was,' Rosie says indignantly. 'It definitely was. I saw her face.'

'Okay, well she could have been here about anything,' Olivia says, yet she hears the doubt in her own voice and her gut tells her that what she says probably isn't true. No one comes to their house, especially not strangers, and her mother can't be trusted, she has always known this. Why was that woman here on Monday, lingering at the end of their road? She said she was waiting for someone, but who could that have been?

Rosie darts from the bed and heads towards the door, and it is only then that Olivia hears their mother's footsteps on the stairs. Moments later, she hears her talking to Rosie, who has managed to make it back to her room without raising suspicion. Olivia needs to think, and fast. She can't do anything while she is still chained to this bed frame, and she can't think of any reason she could use to persuade her mother to let her go. She wishes she had done something before – that she had planned an escape while she was at school – but she always talked herself out of it, too scared of the possible repercussions. What if no one believed her? What if her mother and father managed to persuade the school, the social workers, the police that she was nothing but a troublemaker? She was only fifteen – who would believe a word she said? Now she realises that by waiting, she has made the dangers worse. More than ever, it seems that Rosie is her only lifeline.

She listens. She hears her mother go back downstairs, and then she waits for Rosie to return to her bedroom. 'You need to get out of here,' she tells her. 'Tonight, okay? I need you to get out of the house, but you can't mess it up, all right?'

Rosie is nodding, but she looks terrified. Her eyes are damp with the start of tears and her attention doesn't leave her sister, her gaze focused on her as though she is the only person in the world. The look makes Olivia feel even guiltier. She is the only sane person in Rosie's life; the only person who might have been able to help her, at least. Now she can do nothing, and she hates herself for having failed her sister so spectacularly.

'You know this isn't normal, don't you? What they do to us? You know it doesn't happen to everyone else, don't you?'

Rosie nods again, still muted by fear. Olivia tilts her head towards her, desperate to embrace her in a hug, and Rosie lies down next to her, wrapping her arms around her. They stay like this briefly, knowing the moment must be ended.

'How am I going to do it?' Rosie asks in a whisper.

'We need to distract them. I'll do it. I don't know how yet, but when it happens, you'll just know, okay? We'll have to do it when Dad gets back. It'll be easier for you to get his keys.'

She stops for a moment, trying to formulate a plan. Their father is meticulous in everything he does, but she has noticed a change in him recently. There has been a change in them both. Her parents like to think themselves in control, but from what Olivia has seen, it is slipping from them. Their castle has been infiltrated, their perfect life rocked from the inside out, and all she needs to do is exploit their weaknesses while they're still available. Their fortress is not as impenetrable as they had hoped. All she needs is a moment of carelessness from her father, something overlooked while he's distracted.

Rosie's face has paled. 'I can't do it.'

'You can,' Olivia says, pulling free from her sister's arms. 'Listen to me, you can do this. You *have* to do it. Wait for him to come home – you need to be looking out for him. As soon as he comes through the door, tell him I kicked you. Say you came in here asking to borrow something, and when you came near the bed, I lashed out at you. Make it sound really bad.'

Rosie is shaking her head, silent tears now slipping down her cheeks. 'You'll get in so much trouble.'

'It doesn't matter,' Olivia says, though in truth, the thought of what her father might do to her makes her feel sick. She has tried to ignore it in the past, trying to justify her parents' behaviour to herself to make it seem more ordinary, but she realises now that she has no idea of the extent of her father's potential for violence. And yet a part of her thinks that it can't get any worse. He can beat her if he wants; what does it matter now? If it means she gets to escape this place, the temporary pain will be worth it. She just doesn't want him to hurt Rosie. She wants her sister gone from here, even if it means leaving herself in danger. 'You need to do your best acting for me, okay? Be hysterical. But whatever you do, keep an eye on those keys. Make sure you see what he does with them. And don't take your phone, okay? Just take yourself.'

'Where do I go?'

'Anywhere. Ask someone to take you to the police. But not anyone in this street – try to get further away.'

Rosie wipes the back of a hand over each eye in turn before taking a deep breath. She nods, though the gesture isn't convincing to either of them. Olivia wishes she didn't have to ask for her sister's help. She wishes that she'd spoken to someone sooner, someone who could have come to the house and seen things for what they really were, but there was never a right time, there were never the right words, and she was always too scared of the consequences to confide in anyone about what her life was really like. The fear of the care system – a fear her father has instilled in her and preyed upon regularly over the years – has been enough to deter her from ever speaking out, with the thought of what she and Rosie might face there sufficient to silence her into an almost muted state that for years has made her feel suffocated within her own skin. She hasn't wanted to be separated from Rosie, which has always been the motivation for everything she has and hasn't done.

'You'd better go,' she tells her sister now, and she watches Rosie leave the room without another word, not knowing whether she has helped them or just made things even worse.

TWENTY-THREE

HANNAH

When Michael comes home from work that evening, he is in a terrible mood. Hannah doesn't need to set eyes upon him; she can hear it in the slamming of the front door and his heavy steps upon the stairs when he goes straight to the bedroom to change. When she follows him up, her attempt at a cheery welcome home is greeted by a steely silence.

'Is everything okay?' she asks tentatively. She knows why his mood is so dark. Things with Olivia have escalated far quicker than either of them anticipated. They knew this day would come, that she would push them to a point at which she believes she has her parents broken, and though they have discussed its arrival, neither of them has been prepared for it. Olivia needs to be dealt with, and they should have put a plan in place sooner, she realises that now.

'What did you tell them?'

'The teachers? I told them there's no truth in any of it, obviously. I said we'd been having trouble with her behaviour recently, that she's looking for attention. Neither of them should have been here – I'm sure it's against the rules.'

Michael still has his back to her, but he turns now and steps towards her. His face softens and he smiles, though the look is steeped in a curious kind of sadness, almost disappointment, the kind of look a parent might give an unruly child.

Then his arm is raised and his hand, palm outstretched, is swung towards her. When he slaps her, the shock manages to hit harder than the blow itself. Her own hand flies to her face, shielding the point of impact. In all the years they have been together, he has never raised a hand to her. She has seen him angry – mostly with Olivia – though his anger usually manifests itself in bouts of silence that have at their worst gone on for days. These times have been rare, but Hannah can recall each. Even at his moodiest, though, she has never thought him capable of hitting her.

Yet she is lying to herself, a voice in the back of her head that won't be silenced tells her. She has been lying to herself for years. Perhaps she has always known that the potential for violence was there, rooted in him, and she just never wanted to admit to it.

'Is it really Olivia who's the problem?'

'What do you mean?' she says, her hand still raised to her face.

He smirks at her, a cruel look that she hates to see. She has rarely witnessed him like this, her usually so kind and so patient husband. He loves her, that much she has never doubted. Theirs is a good marriage. They are a team. She is safe here, safe with him; safer than she has ever been anywhere else.

'This is all your fault. You're supposed to look after them.'

Hannah falters on a response. She does look after them; that's all she does. She is here all the time, isn't she, and so are they. She keeps their home immaculate and she ensures that the girls obey the house rules. She has done everything he has asked of her, and yet she can tell from the look on his face that he knows more than he is saying.

'Friday,' he says, as though he needs to prompt her memory. 'Anything you want to tell me?'

She feels sick with the suggestion he is making. He knows, she thinks. He knows that Olivia got out on Friday night, and that she didn't tell him what had happened.

'How …?' she begins, but the question gets stuck in her throat.

Michael smiles, but there is no kindness in the look he gives her. 'You texted me and told me everything was fine, even after I'd asked whether everything was okay. You didn't mention that Olivia had managed to get out of the house, did you?'

Hannah thinks she might be sick. There is a throbbing at her temples and an emptiness in her stomach that burns her from the inside. She thinks of that letter, of everything Carly wrote. She ignored it, not wanting to believe that a word of it could possibly have any basis in reality, and yet now she fears that everything that was written there may be true.

'How did she get out, Hannah?'

'I don't know,' she says, giving the only answer she can. The truth of it is, she still isn't sure. She is always so meticulous with the keys, just as he has taught her to be, but she has been so tired recently, so run down all the time. He has hardly been there to help her, and it's exhausting doing everything by herself, having to deal with the constant drama and the tension that has settled over the house like a suffocating layer of ash. But she can't tell him any of this; he doesn't want to hear it. He will only accuse her of being careless. It will be her fault.

It is her fault.

He is looking at her intently, still waiting for a better answer.

'I went outside to put something in the bin,' she confesses. 'I was gone for seconds, I swear. She must have snuck around the side and waited until I'd gone back in.'

She hates the way he is looking at her, his hazel eyes studying her with such unflinching attention. It was a look she once loved, this long, intense stare, one that said he loved her with the conviction he always so vehemently claimed, but it no longer feels the way it used to, when she was young enough to believe in a happy-ever-after. The way he looked at her, in that way that no one had ever looked at her before, had once felt like a gift, bestowed upon her and no one else, his unflinching attention wrapping her with the comfort of a security blanket. Now, though, restricted within its confines, she finds she is no longer able to breathe.

And yet he is her Prince Charming, she reminds herself, forgetting the sting that lingers beneath the delicate flesh of her cheek. Hasn't he given her the life she craved, a life that before him seemed an impossible dream of escape? She is ungrateful. She has let him down, again.

'I'm sorry,' she tells him, knowing the words will fall on deaf ears. He doesn't want apologies, he wants explanations, but she doesn't have a justifiable one for him no matter how much she wishes she did. She was careless, and there is no excuse for what happened. She should have done better. No matter what she does, she could always have done better.

'So am I. I trusted you to protect the girls, but you don't seem to be able to do that, do you?'

'How did you know she was gone?' Hannah asks, her voice wobbling on the question. She fears the answer, dreading what else she might find out about him. He knows everything, so what else does he know that he hasn't yet mentioned?

Michael laughs and shakes his head. 'You really are an idiot, aren't you? There are trackers on the girls' mobile phones. There's one on yours as well. Do you seriously think I'd let any of you have a phone for any other reason than to keep a check on what you're up to? Just as well I have been, too. You weren't going to tell me a thing, were you?'

He steps closer and leans towards her, his face just inches from hers. 'Liar.'

Hannah gasps involuntarily, the word knocking her sideways. She thinks of the letter, taped to the inside of the lid of one of her shoeboxes inside the wardrobe, wondering whether it is still there. Has he already been back to the house today and managed to find that as well?

She knows it is loaded; the single-word sentence packed with far more meaning than it can speak. Guilt sinks like lead in her stomach, weighing down her guts. She feels sick with the notion of just how wrong she has got things, and for everything she thought Olivia to be capable of. It is a feeling Hannah is familiar with, this awful feeling of regret, but it has never afflicted her in relation to her daughters before. Everything she has done for them she has done with the belief that it has been for the best. Her regrets have only ever applied to her husband, about letting him down when he has done so much for her. It has all been about him: keeping him, loving him, pleasing him.

Yet now she wonders if everything she has seen in front of her has been a lie. She knows there must be some truth in that letter – there are things Carly couldn't possibly have known unless she had had some sort of contact with Michael – and yet she doesn't want to believe it, even now. She won't believe it. Her husband is a good man; he always has been. He saved her when she was at her most vulnerable, when her life would have led her down a path that would have brought her nothing but further misery. If it wasn't for Michael, Hannah hates to think what would have become of her.

'I'm sorry,' she says again, though the word seems to be having no effect. 'I've been so tired recently, and Olivia's behaviour has been so difficult. I just … I let things slip, I know that. It won't happen again, I promise.'

He is silent, and Hannah would rather he shouted at her than let her stew in the terrible quietness that suffocates her.

'Why are you visiting that woman?'

The question is the last one Hannah expects to hear, and yet it makes sense that he knows. Her mouth opens, but she says nothing, aware that further lies would be futile. Michael knows her better than she knows herself; he always has done. It was one of the things that drew her to him when they first met, this way in which he seemed to know what she needed far better than she did. He made decisions for her at times when she didn't want to have to, and she has forever been grateful for it. But this knowing her so well means that he knows when she is lying; he understands so much more than she has ever realised.

He has always referred to her mother as 'that woman'. They never saw eye to eye, not from the first day they met, though it was always obvious why Eleanor objected so strongly to Michael. That hideous man, as she referred to him during one particularly heated row, was going to take Hannah away. Eleanor had moulded her daughter to her liking, keeping her close, shaping her into little more than a slave. She cooked, she cleaned, she did the shopping, and when her mother got sicker, she tended to her physical needs and personal care, receiving nothing but ingratitude and insults along the way, forever reminded of how worthless she was and how her mother could have had so much more from her life had Hannah not been born. No matter how much she did, her efforts were met with nothing but criticism from her mother. Michael was the first and only person to make Hannah realise that the thankless existence she was enduring wasn't normal, and that her mother was controlling her life.

'She's dying,' she tells him.

Michael tuts. It is a cold sound, devoid of empathy, stripped of anything that Hannah might consider human. 'But why bother now? After what she did to you, you're willing to risk everything for her?'

'She's still my mother.'

'She was a useless one, the same as you are now. Do you really think you're any different? You had one job, Hannah – to keep the girls safe. What if something had happened to Olivia on

Friday night? What if she'd got herself into trouble? Whose fault would it be?'

Hannah closes her eyes. She doesn't want to hear the words; she doesn't want to go back there. She knows exactly what he means when he refers to 'trouble'. She has been stupid and foolish – she knows all this. If she could go back and change everything that happened that day, she would, but she can't, and her life is forever tainted by it. She is no better now than she was back then, all those years ago when she was little more than a child, one with still so much to learn.

'How long have you known?'

'Long enough.'

'Then why are you only saying something now?'

Michael sighs and folds his arms across his chest. 'I wanted to see how long you'd keep the pretence up. You've shown just how disloyal you really are.'

Hannah looks away, not wanting to maintain eye contact. Lying has felt wrong – the secret of her visits to her mother has made her uncomfortable – but at no point did she consider that the act might be disloyal. She has only been trying to do her best, for everyone.

'Haven't you learned anything?' he asks, his voice deadened of any emotion.

Hannah looks for her husband in this man: he looks the same, but this can't be him. Michael is the one who was there for her that night, who found her when she didn't answer his calls. He is the one who dressed the wounds that stranger had inflicted upon her body, the one who held her hand and promised that everything was going to be okay. But that man was nothing like the one who stands in front of Hannah now.

'I can't trust you to protect the girls,' he continues. 'You leave your keys in the door. What's the point in having rules if you're just going to flout them? What sort of example is that setting?'

Hannah narrows her eyes. 'You?'

'It's just as well I popped home on Monday to take them out, isn't it? Someone needs to protect you from that woman. Don't you remember what a poisonous old cow she is? I saved you from her once, Hannah … I won't do it a second time.'

He looks as though he is going to say something else, but instead he turns and leaves the room. When she hears him go downstairs, she lies down on the bed, trying to keep her thoughts from what happened that night. But she can't. Every time she closes her eyes, she is dragged back there. The soft mud beneath her that caked her bare legs; the black outlines of the trees against the blue-black of the night sky; the tinny ringing in her head that filled her ears. It all comes back to her, as out of focus now as it was then.

Hours after she was attacked, she woke up in Michael's bed, in the room he rented in a friend's house. She opened her eyes to an Artexed ceiling and a swirl of patterns that made her head hurt and her eyes sting. She was lying beneath a thin sheet that covered the torn and muddied dress she was still wearing, a makeshift dressing on her head. She was safe. He had rescued her. He had told her not to go to that party – he had tried to reason that she had him now, she didn't need to go – but she hadn't listened and had gone anyway. Their relationship – the secrecy, the thrill and promise of it all – had given her a taste of freedom, and like a glutton who hadn't known when she'd had enough to fill her, she had greedily wanted to devour more.

She opens her eyes, unsure how long she has been lying there, lost to the past. The bedroom door is open again, and Michael is standing in the doorway, silently watching her, his eyes burning with fire.

'Where the hell is Rosie?'

TWENTY-FOUR

OLIVIA

Olivia cried when she heard her father come home from work and walk straight up the stairs. Where was Rosie? Why wasn't she doing anything? She waited, but nothing happened. She heard her father go into her parents' bedroom, closing the door after him. She lay in silence, wondering what was going on, knowing that the most likely answer was the one she wanted to contemplate the least. There was nothing going on. Rosie had been too scared and had talked herself out of doing anything that could help them escape this place. Everything was exactly as it always had been.

She lay still until the room grew dark, until her tears had dried upon her face, the sheet beneath her sticking to her with the damp heat of urine. Now she lies in the darkness, her own stench thick in the air around her, and she can't cry any more; there isn't enough fluid left inside her to produce tears. She feels dizzy with dehydration, and she wonders how long she will survive if no one comes to her. There have been so many times when she has thought that dying would be preferable – the silence and solitude of death an appealing prospect against the never-ending regime of her life – but not like this, she thinks. She doesn't want to die alone, handcuffed to her bed.

She has no idea what time it might be when she hears her father call her sister's name; the clock on the far wall of her room, which she knows was put there by her parents to torture her during her long hours of solitary confinement, has stopped, its battery dead. She needs to find sleep, feeling herself exhausted by the strain of the past week, but she is too sad and too angry to close her eyes and allow herself to drift from the waking world. Rosie has let her down in the worst of ways. She knows her little sister is scared, but so is she. This was their chance – perhaps their only chance – but now it is gone, and she mourns it like a living thing, loved and lost.

'Rosie!'

There is a clattering of feet as one of her parents rushes downstairs. The other is on the landing, opening and closing doors, the increased banging suggesting panic and confirming what Olivia has begun to suspect. Rosie has gone. Her heart swells with a flood of anticipation. She hasn't let her down after all; if anything, she has done the opposite. She didn't want Olivia to get hurt, so she has made her own plan, one that doesn't involve her sister. Olivia feels her heart close to bursting with a love that is almost painful, and somehow her body finds itself able to produce tears once again.

The relief that washed over her at the knowledge of her sister's absence is snatched from her by the appearance of her father, who crashes into the room with a face filled with the darkness of the night. He flicks the switch on the bedroom wall, throwing them both into a sudden and oppressive glow of artificial light. There is sweat on his top lip, dark patches beneath the arms of his shirt. The look on his face is one she has seen before, one he tries his best to hide. It never ends well for any of them.

Olivia wants to pretend she isn't scared of him, but she is. She is frightened of both her parents.

'Where's your sister?'

'I don't know.' She pushes herself back on her elbows, struggling to get as far up the bed as she can go, but the cuffs around her ankles stop her. She feels her face flush with shame at the damp patch she is lying in, knowing that her mother will be furious with her when she sees it.

'Liar!'

'I don't know, I swear,' she says, her words coming hurriedly, panicked. 'I've been in here all day.'

She hears her mother coming back up the stairs; a moment later, she is behind her father in the doorway. 'She's not in the garden,' she says quietly.

Her father hasn't taken his eyes from Olivia, not even to acknowledge the presence of her mother behind him. Her parents look at her accusingly, making Olivia feel smaller than they have ever been able to manage before.

'I won't let you ruin everything,' he says softly, his voice low and taunting. Yet there is something in his eyes, something that contradicts his words and the tone in which they are spoken. They are glassy and tired, an unspoken and inadvertent admission that Olivia has managed to unsettle him more than he would ever admit. He turns to Hannah and snaps his fingers. She fumbles in her pocket and passes him a set of keys. 'You're coming with me.'

He reaches for Olivia's right ankle and unlocks the cuff. A flood of feeling rushes up her leg as the blood flows freely and she can move it properly. All she really wants to do is kick out, catch her father off guard and run from this room and this house. She knows she can't; she would never make it. Even if she managed to get past him, her mother is right behind him. Sometimes she is more scared of her mother than she is of her father. There is something so unnatural about the way Hannah treats her daughters, and her coldness manages to make her menacing. She is nothing like a mother should be, or what Olivia believes a mother should be. All the niceness she has ever displayed, all those hours spent playing the role of the doting mother, has been a pretence, as though she has had to force herself to believe that she is happy here with this life they have built around them and barricaded themselves inside.

'Where are you taking her, Michael?'

'Shut up. Isn't this what you wanted?'

Michael unlocks the cuffs that bind Olivia's wrists. As with her leg, she feels a rush of sensation that sweeps back into her arms, offering her a momentary hope that she might be able to find some way out of here. When her father unlocks her left ankle, she stands slowly, not wanting to give the impression of an imminent attempt at escape. She would never risk it; she couldn't do it. She feels sick and weak, her body drained of all its energy and reserves.

'Try anything and you'll only make things worse,' her father warns her.

Olivia wonders just how much worse things can possibly get, but she looks to her mother, a glance that pleads for help, desperately searching for a possible common ground between them somewhere. Her mother responds with nothing, seeming dead behind the eyes. She isn't natural, Olivia thinks. Everything about her is wrong.

'You can't tell me what to do,' Olivia says, feeling a hot flush rise in waves through her. She glances to her mother again before meeting Michael's eye. 'You're not even my father.'

He turns from Olivia to Hannah, the colour rushing to his face in a vivid burst of scarlet. 'What have you told her?'

She sees the flood of panic that washes over her mother's face, draining her skin of colour. She must have known he would find out that Olivia had discovered the truth. Had she really wanted to, Hannah could have kept it hidden for longer. She didn't have to speak. She could have kept the secret from Olivia for the rest of her life if necessary, and yet she chose not to, and now Olivia wonders why. She must surely have known that he would react in only one way, so why did she do it? Has she finally realised that all this has gone too far?

'She just found out,' Hannah splutters, stumbling over her words.

'Just found out. Just found out how?'

Her father's voice is low and controlled; everything Olivia knows they should both be fearful of. She has heard this voice enough times to know that nothing good ever follows it.

Hannah's eyes flit between Michael and Olivia. She isn't going to mention the diary, Olivia thinks; she has managed to keep its existence a secret from him for this long, and even now she can't bring herself to just tell the truth. She is protecting herself first, above all else.

'Found out how?' her father repeats, his voice louder now.

Her mother glances at her again, sending Olivia an unspoken communication she is unable to read.

'She … I …'

But she has no answer, and even if she could find one, her response is too slow for Michael's liking. His arm is raised so suddenly, his hand flung forward so quickly, that neither Olivia nor Hannah has time to react. The back of his hand meets Hannah's face with an awful crack, and when she falls back, her head hits the corner of Olivia's wooden chest of drawers. She falls to the floor, her left cheek pressed to the carpet, where a small trail of blood appears from the back of her head, a tiny river of red on the beige wool.

'Mum!'

'Come on!' Michael grabs Olivia by the arm, ignoring her protests.

'You need to get her help!'

'Shut up!'

He pushes her out onto the landing and down the stairs. She has been in her room, lying in that bed, for so long now that it is as though her legs have forgotten how they are supposed to work;

she feels as if there is quicksand beneath her, pulling her down, and she wobbles and stumbles as she is bumped down each step.

She screams as her father pulls her past the living room doorway and along the hallway. Her cries for help are met with a clip to the side of the head as he opens the door to the garage and takes her through to the car. Olivia can't remember how long it has been since she was last in the garage. She and Rosie are banned from ever entering it – not that either of them would come to this place out of choice. They are only ever brought here when punishment is involved, and the hours she has spent locked in the boot of her father's estate have been the longest and loneliest of her life, a painful reminder of who is in charge and who they are to obey.

The garage smells of petrol, and years of dust catch in her throat, choking her cries for help.

'I said shut up!'

She feels the blow to the head, a sharp crack that sends her reeling. She watches the dark room fall to blackness as her vision leaves her. Her cries fall silent as her limp body is bundled into the boot of the car.

TWENTY-FIVE

HANNAH

'Hannah! Hannah, can you hear me?'

There is a white noise in her head and an awful searing pain that grips her skull. Hannah opens her eyes, trying to concentrate her vision on a single point, but everything is moving in front of her, shifting out of focus as though she is looking through water. She knows this feeling; she has been here before, years ago. She recognises the pain that swells in her brain and knows that she has been hit on the head; then everything comes rushing back to her with blinding accuracy. The girls, she thinks. Where are the girls?

'Hannah, my name is Gary. We're going to get you on this stretcher, okay?'

'I'm fine,' she says, knocking away the hand that rests on her arm. She is not fine, but she doesn't need their help. She needs to find her daughters. She needs to find Michael. She knows what it is to feel fear for herself, but now she understands just how overpowering love for your children can be. Despite everything, she does love the girls; surely everyone will realise that. She has only ever wanted to protect them, to keep them safe from all the bad things that this world will try to throw at them.

'No!' she cries, as another paramedic tries to lift her from behind. 'I said stop it!'

She pushes herself up on an arm, trying to right herself and put her thoughts into order, all the while attempting to force back the searing pain that clutches her temples. Michael has taken Olivia. She never meant for this to happen, but it is all her fault, she knows that. She hasn't wanted to accept what her husband is, and just what he might be capable of, but now she is being forced to, and she knows that it will come at a price. They will all pay in some way for whatever it is he plans to do.

She sits up. The paramedics are exchanging looks above her head.

'We need to take you to hospital, Hannah,' the one called Gary is saying.

She stands, though doing so makes her sway, the bedroom shifting out of focus around her. She feels a hand on her arm trying to steady her, but with a shove she frees herself of it and stumbles out onto the landing. There is something she needs to find; something she needs to see again. The letter. She needs to see that letter. Could she have been so wrong all this time? Was she really that naïve, so lonely and so desperate to be loved that she allowed herself to fall into a trap that would become her entire life?

She goes into her own bedroom, ignoring the protests of the paramedics, who follow her out onto the landing. Someone else is coming up the stairs, a woman wearing a police uniform, and Hannah darts into the bedroom, locking the door behind her. She goes to the wardrobe and scrabbles about on its floor, searching for the shoebox and the letter that is still taped inside.

'Mrs Walters!' The police officer is knocking on the bedroom door. 'Mrs Walters, you need to let me in!'

With shaking hands, Hannah unfolds the letter. She has only read it once, yet that was enough for the contents to seep deep into her brain, marking her with a stain she knows is permanent. She wanted to ignore it, but she knows she can't do so any longer.

Dear Hannah,

You don't know me, but my name is Carly. I have been having an affair with your husband for the past two years. We met in a bar and things just went from there. I thought he loved me, but I realise now how wrong I was. When we met, I didn't know that he was married or that he had children. I found out about six months after we started seeing each other, when he convinced me that the marriage was on the rocks, that you were already living separate lives and it was just a matter of time before he left you to be with me. By the time I found out about you, he had me hooked. I loved him and I believed that despite his secrets, he loved me. He promised to look after me and my son. I thought he meant it.

There are things I need to tell you, things I've done that I'm not proud of. Michael can be very persuasive, and I realise now just how brainwashed I have been by him. I broke into your home. I wish I hadn't done it, but Michael asked me to, and just days ago I would have done anything he asked of me. I would have believed anything he said. He told me that he couldn't explain the situation to me yet – he said he would tell me everything when we were together properly. He said you'd done things that had let him down, and he wanted to leave but he needed to do it without hurting the girls. He told me that doing what he asked me to would make it easier for him to leave; that the sooner I did it, the sooner we could be together, a proper family. He wouldn't explain why he wanted me to do what I did in your kitchen, but he said that you had done bad things, things he wanted you to know weren't a secret any more. He convinced me that you were the liar, but I should have seen long ago that the only liar is Michael.

There is something else, too. Michael asked me to call you and pretend to be someone from your daughter's school. I wasn't happy with it – what he was asking didn't seem right – but he kept on at me, saying it was the only way we would get to be together. He told me that you were a danger to the girls, that you didn't treat them well, that he wanted you to feel the way you had made them feel. He promised me it would be the last thing he would ask of me, but after I'd done it, I realised he wasn't going to leave you. Trusting him has been the biggest mistake of my life.

I told Michael that I knew he was never planning to be with me and that I was going to tell you everything. And then he raped me. I'm sorry just to come out with it, but there's no other way to tell you. Afterwards, he told me that I couldn't go to the police – that there was evidence of our affair and that once they had my DNA, I could be linked to the break-in at your house. He said that if I told anyone what had happened, no one would believe me; that I would look like a jealous girlfriend trying to get revenge after being rejected. He said that if I was arrested for the break-in, my son would be taken away from me, and I am too scared that he is right to risk it.

Please destroy this letter after you've read it. I am scared of Michael and what he is capable of, what he might do if he finds this, but you need to know who you are married to. I am covered in bruises, but none of them in places where they can be seen. Michael is far too clever for that, isn't he? He only allows people to see what he wants them to see. It's only now that I realise how manipulative and controlling he is. You need to protect yourself and your daughters. I'm sorry for everything I've done, I really

am, but please don't ignore what I'm telling you. You have
to get away from him. Michael is dangerous.

Carly

Hannah ignores the sound of the fist being beaten against the
locked bedroom door and the repetition of her name as it is shouted
over and over by the police officer out on the landing. She knows
it is only a matter of time before the door is broken open and she
is taken away, and then all her secrets will be spread beyond the
safety of this house, there for everyone to criticise and judge her
by. She closes her eyes and pictures the young woman who stood
on her doorstep just days ago, focusing on the details of her face,
the lost, faraway look that was ingrained in the deep brown of
her eyes. Surely it isn't possible for someone to be so naïve as this
Carly claims herself to have been. If everything she says is true,
she would have seen Michael for what he really was a long time
ago, wouldn't she?

With her eyes still closed, the face in front of Hannah changes,
merging into another, this one far more familiar to her. She raises
a hand to the back of her head, touching the soft flesh of her skull,
split and bloodied. She feels hot tears escape her closed eyes, and
as the bedroom door is forced open and a wave of noise hits the
silence that has in these moments gripped her, she looks back at
her younger self, not wanting to recognise her.

TWENTY-SIX
OLIVIA

Olivia wakes to the sound of a car engine, and to a bumping, lurching movement that shudders her into consciousness. She is submerged in darkness, and when she puts her hands out to either side of her, they are met with the coldness of metal. Everything comes rushing back to her, images of the evening that has just passed hurtling through her mind like oversized hailstones raining down upon her, so big and so fast they threaten to knock her out once again. Her head fills with a pain that is new to her, more powerful than any other she has ever experienced. She feels sick. Where is Rosie? She prays to someone she has never believed in that wherever her sister might be, she is safe.

When she screams, her voice makes hardly a sound. Her throat is raw and the breath in her lungs is ragged and broken, barely there at all. She puts both hands flat to the lid of the boot and bangs against it with all the energy she has left in her frail and tortured body. Her wrists still throb from the cuts made by the cuffs, and a lack of food and drink has weakened her, making her even more light-headed. She wants to cry, but she is past that now; she knows that she must conserve what little energy she has left for whatever comes next.

Why didn't she do it before? she thinks. She could have contacted the police a long time ago, or walked into Miss Johnson's classroom one lunchtime and just told her what was going on. But there was never the right time. There were never the right words. She didn't want to admit what her life really was; she didn't want to be ripped from everything she knew, no matter how bad those things were. Writing it down felt like admitting it without actually having to do so, as though in the act of writing she was delivering someone else's truth, never having to acknowledge or accept that this was her. This was her life.

She wishes now that she had done it sooner, but she understands the futility of wishes, knowing that she has never been able to rely upon them in the past, no matter how much she might have put her faith in their possibilities. The truth is, she loves her parents. She hates what they do to her and to Rosie and she hates how their treatment of her makes her feel, yet she cannot help but love them because they are all she knows. She wants them to be different, to be the kind of parents that as a little girl she would imagine herself having. For years she believed that they would change, that one day something would make them see things differently and they would stop all this. They would be a happy family, the kind Olivia has always wanted to be a part of.

She knows differently now. Her parents can't change. This is who they are.

The fear of the unknown has kept Olivia silent; the uncertainty of social services and care homes and separation from her sister enough to convince her that she might be better off enduring the treatment of the devil she knows. What would her life become if everyone knew the truth about her family and the way they live? She and Rosie would never be able to escape it, and though they have been trapped in one place, she feared that an exposure of the truth would see them caught somewhere else, somewhere neither of them would have any chance of leaving.

It isn't long before the car comes to a stop and the engine is cut. She hears Michael get out and slam the door, and a moment later the boot is opened. She kicks out desperately, flailing her limbs in a bid to fight back against her father. But he is too strong and his movements too swift, and she is pulled from the boot as though she is weightless.

Once out of the cramped space, she attempts to make out the shapes around her. They are outside, somewhere open and windy, though it is so dark that she feels she may as well still be in the boot of the car. Her bare feet are on damp grass, cold and scratchy against the soles of her feet. A keen breeze whips at her hair, raising tiny goose bumps along her skinny arms.

Her father holds her by the scruff of her pyjama top, his other arm wrapped around her chest. She writhes to try to free herself, but his grip on her tightens, and when he begins to move, she finds herself lifted from the ground, her attempts to free herself all in vain. The weight she has lost during the past year is making this easier for him; she doesn't know, as she has never checked, but she can't weigh much more than a hundred pounds. He carries her as though she is a doll, his efforts made easier still by her lethargy and lack of reserves.

'You won't get away with this,' she shouts as she struggles to free herself, still not wanting to dwell on whatever 'this' might be. She knows that it is all over now; that things have gone too far for her parents to continue to get away with what they have been doing. Rosie will have raised the alarm by now. Whoever she tells will go to the house looking for Olivia, and they will find her mother there. She wonders whether Hannah is alive or dead, and the thought that her father has killed her hits her with a sudden blow, like a punch to the side of the head. She knows she shouldn't care, but she does. Despite everything she has done – despite everything she hasn't done – Hannah is her mother. Olivia wants to believe that this still counts for something, though the last thread of hope she clings to is one that is frayed nearly to the point of snapping loose.

'You're a girl who exposed herself to half the school, and now you're all over the internet. The shame was too much – you couldn't take it any more.'

Michael's words are cold and detached – they echo in the empty space that is vast around them – but there is something in his voice that betrays them, some shakiness that tells Olivia he doesn't mean everything he says. There is a break at the edge of every syllable, a crack of uncertainty, each word as fragile as an eggshell, easily broken. Whatever he is planning to do, she thinks, he doesn't really want to do it. Yet he is going to do it anyway. Perhaps he sees no other way out, and Olivia realises that for him, at least, there isn't one.

In the distance, her eyes now attuned to the darkness that surrounds her, she makes out the sight of the pier on which she stood just days ago. It is lined with tiny golden lights that glow in the darkness like a string of flickering fireflies. It is beautiful here, she thinks. It is frightening how much darkness can lurk behind the closed doors of somewhere so close to such loveliness.

'Don't do this,' she says, her own words broken.

She feels sick. She has wanted to be noticed, for someone to realise that something isn't right with her and the life she has been living, but everything she has done this past week has made things easier for him. Will anyone even miss her? she wonders.

Rosie. The thought of her sister is enough to pull her from her self-pity, from the notion that whatever his plans are, he can't do anything to her that she doesn't now embrace the thought of, and with a desire to live that shocks her with its ferocity, she lowers her head and sinks her teeth into the bare flesh of her father's lower arm. She bites so hard that she breaks his skin, and as she tastes with a dizzying mix of disgust and fury the metallic tang of his blood, he cries out and stumbles. As he loses his footing, Olivia writhes from his grip and runs.

'You little bitch!'

He is already too close, and Olivia steps on something sharp and stinging, something that slices the sole of her foot and makes her scream out in pain. She runs through the burning sensation that threatens to slow her down and hold her back – she thinks she may have stepped on a piece of broken glass, though she doesn't allow her mind to linger on the possibility for too long in case it should slow her escape – but too soon she feels him behind her, and there is nothing she can do when he pulls her legs from beneath her.

'You're nothing but a little tart,' he says breathlessly, as her body slams to the ground. 'You're just like your mother was. It would be better for us both if you weren't mine.'

The words hit Olivia with the force of a truck, far worse than any physical assault he could launch upon her. She forgets the pain in her foot, as well as the new, searing agony that has lit a flame along the length of her left arm, bent beneath her. The breath has been knocked from her lungs by his words. Behind her, ragged among his awful words and his deafening rage, she can hear something else. He is crying, his sobs tangled in the hatred he feels for her.

'What?' she manages, speaking the word into the ground, barely hearing the sound its single syllable makes. Is Michael her father after all? Did her mother get the timings wrong? She knew she looked too much like him not to be his daughter, though as far as she is concerned, this is where the similarities end. She is nothing like him. She will never allow herself to be anything like him.

He says nothing, but drags her up again, heaving her like a bag of cement. He is struggling now, his energies as depleted as hers. He drops her onto her feet in front of him, fighting to get his breath back, and Olivia turns to him. She catches the glint of his eyes in the darkness, the dampness that sits at their corners, giving the false impression that he is human despite everything, but it is too little and too late, and she doesn't believe it. They are actors, her parents, having trained for years in the roles they have created for themselves.

'I've tried my best for you,' he says, his voice breathless, his breathing ragged. 'Everything I've done has been for you girls, but it's never been enough, has it?'

His words are a repetition of everything that's been fed to her by her mother, yet Olivia realises that the opposite is true: this is her father's mantra, drummed into Hannah until she started to believe it as the truth. What they have done has never been about Olivia or Rosie; it has been about him and about their mother, satisfying some perverse desire for control. Her parents are sick, trapped in this tiny bubble of a world they have created for themselves, convincing themselves that they are right and that it is everyone else who is wrong.

'It isn't normal,' she says through her tears. 'We're not normal.'

'We're as normal as anyone else,' he argues, his voice filled with frustration. 'What does it matter to you what everyone else is doing? You've had the best of everything all your life, even when you haven't deserved it. Why can you never be happy with what you've got?'

'You're mad,' Olivia says, straightening herself and clutching her arm. The pain is reaching her shoulder now, a burning that courses through her chest. 'You'll never get away with this. Everyone will know what you are – Rosie will make sure of it.'

Her father titters as though she has said something amusing, but she manages even in the darkness to see the flicker of panic that darts across his eyes, if only for the briefest of moments. The life he planned so thoroughly and put into practice with such care and control is falling apart around him, and this time there is nothing he can do to stop it from happening. He must have known it couldn't last forever, that at some point one of them would try to break free.

Of course he did, she thinks, and he always knew that of the two of them, it would be Olivia who would do it. Perhaps this is the real reason why both her parents have always hated her so much.

'Are you my father?' she asks. Though she knows it shouldn't matter now – that all that should matter is surviving this night and finding Rosie – it does. She needs to know the truth about where she came from.

When he nods without speaking, a silent admission manages to make itself present between them. For the first time, Olivia realises what he is saying: not that her mother had the timings wrong, but that he was the rapist. She tastes bile in the back of her throat as the truth fills her head with its horror, its taste thick and sour, and her ears ring with the scream of the breeze as it cuts against her skin. This can't be what he means, she thinks. It can't be him. Amid the chaos of her thoughts, another creeps into her head, slowly and methodically, a parasite. Does her mother know that it was Michael who raped her?

A face flashes before her, its presence so vivid that it is almost as though the woman stands before her now, her eyes pleading with her. She blinks her away, not wanting to think about that woman at the end of their street, or the little boy who looked at her with such hopelessness, as though he was silently willing her to help them. She was there for Michael, she thinks; that's who she was waiting for, and that's why she stopped Olivia. She must have known who she was. Perhaps she didn't need to know the time at all; maybe it was just an excuse to talk to her.

Didn't Rosie say her body had been found on the beach near here?

'What did you do to her?' she asks. If she dies tonight, she wants to hear the truth before she goes, no matter how chilling it might be. None of it makes sense to her, but if what she now suspects turns out to be real, and her father raped her mother, then he is surely capable of anything. Rosie's words come back to her. She sees the young woman's face again, and she believes now that her sister didn't make a mistake. She was there, at their house. She wanted to make herself known to them.

'That woman on the television,' she says, as though her father needs prompting. 'The one they found on the beach. Was it you?'

She screams again as her father lunges for her, and any glimmer of humanity she might have witnessed in his eyes just moments ago is gone. He pushes her towards the cliff edge that drops sheer in front of them, and the sound of her cry becomes tiny, stolen by the wind and thrown to the great expanse of sea that stretches below.

'I'm sorry, Liv,' he says, grappling with her as she tries to fight him. 'I've tried to do my best by you, but you've made it impossible.'

She screams again, but there is no one to hear her. She wriggles frantically and manages to free herself, but when she tries to run, he is once again too quick for her, and she knows that what little strength she has left in her body is fading fast. He grips her again, pushing her back towards the edge. He is so strong, and she is so tired, with nothing more than the will to live to use against him. Yet it surprises her just how powerful that will to live is.

She drops down suddenly, as though she has slipped or tripped over something. Her father lunges forward as she falls, but manages to steady himself. His grasp on her shoulders is lost, and Olivia winces in pain as she lands on her already injured arm. She reaches out and clasps something cold and hard, and as her father reaches down to grab her again, her hand swings up from the ground in one swift, precise motion. There is a dull thud as the rock slams against his skull. He groans in pain, staggers back and falls to the ground.

Olivia scrambles to her feet, not daring to look back at him as she flees. The noise of the wind fills her ears and the smell of the sea lingers in the air around her. There is grass beneath her feet and open space ahead of her, and her legs pump harder than they ever have, and on the tip of her tongue is the taste of the night.

TWENTY-SEVEN

HANNAH

Two weeks have passed since Hannah was arrested. She has been denied bail. Until now, both of her daughters have refused to see her. She hasn't had any contact with Michael, though she knows what he tried to do to Olivia. He is trying to claim that everything is his wife's fault, that she manipulated him into keeping the girls in the house and denying them a normal life. Perhaps it is true. After everything that has happened, Hannah doesn't know what or who to believe. She can't trust herself. She can't trust anyone.

What is normal, anyway? The girls have been fed and clothed. They are clean and healthy. They go to school. Hasn't she been doing just what every parent is expected to do, trying to bring her children up in the best way she sees fit? Rules are there for a reason, for good reason if they are fair and implemented properly. Schools have them – why shouldn't she? If she had listened to good sense when she was younger, so much might have been avoided. She paid for her mistakes. She knows that one day Olivia will pay for hers, too.

She waits in what has been described as the family liaison room, though she knows that whatever happens between her and Olivia today, a liaison is the last thing she expects. Olivia wanted to be free from her. Now she has her wish. She glances at the woman sitting silently in the corner of the room, an officer who has been sent here to oversee the meeting. She has been told there will also be a social worker present. She wants to explain so many things to Olivia, but there are subjects she doesn't want to be forced to talk about in front of these women.

When Olivia enters the room, she looks so different to the girl she was just two weeks earlier. There is more colour in her cheeks, and she seems to have put a bit of weight on in just this short space of time. She avoids eye contact with Hannah, instead glancing to the woman who follows in behind her. There is no sign of Rosie.

'Liv.'

Olivia ignores the sound of her name, but sits down at the table opposite Hannah. She puts her hands on the table and picks at her nails distractedly. The social worker takes a seat next to the policewoman; something is muttered between them, but Hannah doesn't hear what is said.

'Mum,' Olivia says eventually.

The look passed between them is impossible for Hannah to read. She has doubted for so long that she knows her older daughter; now she must surrender to the fact that she doesn't know her at all. She may have the same parentage as Rosie, but she is still a different creature altogether.

'How have you been?'

Olivia nods, but says nothing.

'And Rosie?'

'She's fine.' Olivia looks at her now, holding her gaze with an attention that makes Hannah feel uncomfortable. 'Why did you do it?'

Hannah exhales softly, knowing that however she chooses to answer that question, Olivia will fail to understand. She could never understand. Her eyes are steely, seeking explanation. Her jaw is tightened as though to stop herself from crying. Hannah doesn't want to see her cry. She has never wanted to see either of her daughters crying, no matter what people might be saying about her. On the television and in the newspapers they are calling her a monster. Unnatural.

But no one knows what her life has been like or why she has lived the way she has.

'I thought I was doing what was best. I only ever wanted to protect you.'

It isn't the answer Olivia wants. She looks frustrated; angry, even. 'From what? From being normal?'

'I never wanted what had happened to me to happen to you. That's why I was so upset that night you went to the party. I'd snuck out, Olivia, just like you – I've told you what happened. I've always told you how alike we are. I didn't want to see history repeat itself.'

'In case I got pregnant and lumbered with a child I hated?'

The words are unnecessary and unfair, but Hannah knows they have been uttered with the intention of hurting her. 'I don't hate you. I've never hated you.'

But Olivia doesn't believe it. Her silence says as much.

'They told me you and Rosie are with the same foster family. Are they nice?'

Olivia nods. 'You remember Miss Johnson?' she asks, and Hannah feels a knot form in her chest, tightening around her heart and threatening to cut her breath. 'She has relatives who foster. We're staying with them for a while.'

There is a look in her daughter's eye that lets Hannah know her words have been designed to cause injury, and she wonders for a moment whether she is telling the truth. Olivia must surely realise what she thinks of that teacher, the woman her daughter chose to share her secrets with.

She doesn't respond, not wanting to give Olivia the satisfaction of knowing she has hurt her.

'Do you remember that story you used to tell me,' Olivia says after a while, sitting back and folding her arms across her chest.

'The one about the monster who comes into the house when the windows haven't been locked at night?'

Hannah nods.

'It terrified me for months.'

There was a good reason for the story, which Olivia knows perfectly well. It wasn't Hannah's intention to scare her without reason, but Olivia was always questioning things, forever demanding to know 'why this?' and 'why that?'. Better for her to have a few months of nightmares than a real one that would stay with her and haunt her for life.

'I did what I thought was best.'

Olivia leans across the table, shooting a look at the women in the far corner. She lowers her voice to a whisper. 'You locked us in with the monster.'

Hannah feels dizzy with sickness. Despite everything that has happened, she still doesn't want to believe that the man who raped her that night all those years ago was the same man who then turned up to save her and rescue her from her life. She had met him not long before, just a few months earlier, and he had given her a confidence she had never thought she was capable of. He made her see things differently, offering her the promise of something better. New things seemed possible; a normal life was all she had ever wanted. He had asked her not to go to that party, but she had never really been to one before and she couldn't see what harm there was in it. Everyone else was doing it; why did she always have to be the outsider? She had just wanted to be like the other girls, to get dressed up and get drunk, to lose herself and her life for a few hours.

It seems impossible to Olivia that Hannah couldn't have known it was him, and yet they had never had sex before; that had happened for the first time five months after the attack, with him never putting pressure on her for any kind of intimacy. She didn't recognise him, not in the darkness and with the blow to the head. She couldn't have known it was him.

'I swear to you I didn't know what he was.'

Olivia shakes her head. 'Yes you did. You must have. No one can be that naïve – you must have realised all along, you just didn't want to accept it. How did you think you were going to keep us there forever?'

Hannah doesn't have the answers Olivia seems so desperately to crave. Olivia hasn't lived Hannah's life; she could never understand where she came from and what it meant to her to be freed. Michael wasn't a monster, not always. The man she met was kind and compassionate and generous. Her mother warned her of the age gap, of how quickly Hannah was allowing things to move, but she didn't want to hear any of it. Her mother only wanted to keep her to herself. No one would have been good enough because any man would have been regarded as a threat.

'I didn't know about that girl. I never thought he was capable of anything like that, I swear to you.'

'That girl's name was Carly,' Olivia points out, as though Hannah needs reminding of the fact. 'And you didn't think he was capable of anything like what? Anything like murder, you mean? Just say it. For once, just speak the truth.'

Hannah shakes her head. She knows it is true, but she still doesn't want to hear it. Rapist … murderer … husband. Everything she thought she knew is a lie. He found her when she was at her most vulnerable, just as he did with Carly, and he lured her with the promise of security. When she closes her eyes, that evening comes back to her like a recurring nightmare, the outlines shifting into focus with every replay of the memory. It was him – she knows now that it was him. Perhaps somewhere, in a part of her brain she has trained herself to shut down, she has always known.

'I set you free, didn't I?'

Olivia's face contorts at the comment, as though she has no idea what her mother is talking about.

'Telling you about the rape. I didn't have to. I knew you wouldn't keep it to yourself – I knew you'd tell your father. I did that for you, Olivia.'

'You did it for yourself, you mean. You knew everything was coming to an end, didn't you? You couldn't keep our secrets forever, so you did what you could to make yourself look innocent.'

Hannah shakes her head. Olivia is wrong, about everything. She loves her; she must realise that. She has only wanted to keep her safe. She has tried to do that in the best and only way she has ever known, yet it has never been good enough for her daughter.

Olivia sits back and something in her face changes. She looks at Hannah with such sadness that it is almost as though she has aged a decade in those few moments. Hannah is no longer looking at a child. She is looking at a young woman, someone who knows far more than her years might suggest.

'It wasn't your fault.'

'What wasn't?' Hannah asks, in the vain hope that her daughter might excuse all the sins of which she knows she is guilty.

'The rape. You said something before, something about wearing too little. You made it sound as though it was your fault, like you'd been asking for it. You weren't.'

They sit in silence. Hannah doesn't know what to say. It has always felt to her as though it *was* her fault, as though some God she was always unsure of anyway was punishing her for betraying her duty to her mother and for then disobeying Michael's request. He hadn't wanted her to go to that party. All he had ever done was try to protect her. She let him down.

'Did you know it was him?'

'No. Of course I didn't.'

But Olivia is looking at her with scepticism, her young face filled with doubt. The same doubt sits in Hannah's mind, gnawing away at her what remains of her sanity. Did she know? Was there ever something, anything, that might have made her question just who Michael was and exactly what he was capable of? If there had been, she knows she chose to ignore it.

'Why didn't you go to the police?'

She presses her fingertips to her eyelids. She knew the question was coming, and though she has been over and over it with herself, she realises it will never sound credible to anyone else. Carly might have understood it, she thinks. She and anyone else Michael might have done this to, because Hannah feels sure now that there will have been others. She thinks about how he was there for her in the days and weeks that followed that night. He was the only person she confided in; she could never have told her mother what had happened. Michael consoled her, comforted her, waited for her until she was ready. His real character was kept hidden behind a facade of concern and respectability, and now Hannah wonders how many other women – how many other girls – have fallen for the act.

'I was drunk,' she says, as though everything can be explained away with such simplicity. 'I went out dressed like I was asking for it. Who would have taken me seriously?'

Olivia's expression says that she knows these are not Hannah's words; that they have come from someone else. 'He convinced you not to go to the police, didn't he?'

Hannah shakes her head. 'It's more complicated than it sounds,' she tells her, still protecting him. 'I was from the wrong estate – no one would have paid any attention to a girl like me. That's where our lives are so different, can't you see? I had nothing. You've been given everything.'

Olivia narrows her eyes. Hannah hates the look she is giving her, defiant and filled with contempt. She wants to believe that her mother is evil, that everything is her fault, and Hannah suspects that this is what she will continue to believe regardless of what she tells her. All these people – the police, the social workers, her teachers – are helping to fill Olivia's head with the nonsensical notion that she and Rosie are the victims of some sort of abuse, but none of them knows the truth, and Hannah can sleep at night in the knowledge that she has only ever been a good mother to her girls. She isn't responsible for her husband's sins, no matter how much they may want to try to pin the blame upon her.

'This is what he told you, isn't it?' Olivia says. 'And you've repeated it to yourself so many times over the years that you believe it's all true. Someone would have listened to you. Someone would have believed you.'

She is staring at her with such contempt that Hannah looks down to avoid it. She doesn't know what Olivia wants to hear from her; she only knows that what she is telling her now is all she has.

'All these nice things you've been so keen to possess,' Olivia says, continuing to eye her mother with cynicism. 'The show home and everything just so. What's the point of a spotless house that no one ever gets to visit? Or have you just been trying to scrub something clean for all these years?'

When Hannah gives no response to either question, Olivia sits back in her chair with her arms folded across her chest. 'He brainwashed you, didn't he? He saw you had nothing and he promised you everything, just like he did with Carly.'

Hannah hears the truth like a klaxon in her head, the sounding of a warning bell that she should have heard so many years ago. She knows that Michael did to her what he went on to do to that poor girl whose body was found on the beach, the only difference being that Carly was cleverer than Hannah, smart enough to see what he was doing. But not before it was too late. Just as with that girl, everything he orchestrated with Hannah was premeditated. Nothing happened by chance.

'He told me that few rapists are ever caught. He said that once people knew about it, I'd get a reputation and I'd never be able to get rid of it. The thought of my mother finding out horrified me, so when I discovered I was pregnant, he took me away, somewhere I could have you without her ever knowing. I was only seventeen, Olivia, I didn't know any different. I believed he wanted what was best for me.'

Olivia looks down at her hands. 'Just like you both told me I could never tell anyone about the locks on the windows and the cuffs on the bed because Rosie and I would be separated?'

When she looks up, it is Hannah's turn to look away. She feels a shame of some sort, of course she does, though it is difficult to identify when it feels so alien to her. She allowed Michael to convince her that Olivia was responsible for the strange things that had been going on – the break-in at the house, the phone call to the school. Her mind was so confused that she even believed her daughter was responsible for the missing keys, that she had come home from school to move them. She feels an element of regret for her suspicions, though anyone would be forgiven for assuming the worst of Olivia, given all else she was guilty of. It makes sense now why Michael instructed her to go to Olivia's room on Saturday evening, despite them having already agreed that she would remain shackled to the bed for the night. He wanted her freed so that she could then appear guilty of the crime he had orchestrated with another woman, one as blind to his true nature as Hannah has been.

Above all else, stronger than any other feeling that may have passed through her during these past couple of weeks, is the conviction that she only ever did what she thought was best, as any mother would. The girls weren't hurt; they were never beaten. Whenever Olivia was restrained, it was usually for her own safety, to stop her doing anything that might end up hurting her. She has never known what is best for her, not in the way that her parents do. The authorities are accusing Hannah of child abuse, but nothing could be further from the truth. Her children have been kept safe and sheltered, clean and fed. They haven't been abused, not physically and not sexually. They were safe. No one knows their children like a mother does. No one can look after them like she can.

'Your mother used to hit you, didn't she? It says so in the diary.'

'All the time,' Hannah says too quickly, reaching out for what appears to her to be a lifeline. 'If I didn't do what she'd told me … if I was too slow to get something done. Sometimes I think she did it just because she could.' She sits forward and reaches across the table, but Olivia withdraws from the touch of her mother's fingers against her skin. They have never been physically close; now, apparently, it's far too late for that.

'You see,' Hannah continues, 'I've done everything I can to give you a better life than the one I had. I've never hit you, have I?'

Olivia looks at her incredulously. 'You kept me chained to a bed,' she says, her voice flat and emotionless. 'You kept me overweight so that no one would ever look at me with anything but pity. There's more than one type of abuse.'

'I wanted to keep you safe.'

'By keeping me fat and frightened?' She fires the words across the table. 'By making sure I never had any friends and that no one wanted to know me?' She pauses and takes a deep breath. 'If your mother was really so awful to you, then why wouldn't you have done everything you could to be better? If she was such a terrible mother, why didn't you try to be a good one? If you hadn't let *him* dictate,' she continues, spitting the word as though just thinking her father's name is more than she can stomach, 'we could have been happy, just the three of us, but all you've done is the same as your own mother did: control and manipulate.'

Hannah feels as though she has been slapped. Her daughter's words crush her. Is this what Olivia thinks, that everything has been so bad? Has she really been such an awful mother? She can remember happy times. All those hours she spent playing with her daughter, trying to force a love that had never come naturally to her. She thought herself convincing for the most part. She did her best.

'I've given you all I could,' she says.

'Except you haven't. Because even now, you can't bring yourself to say sorry, can you? You don't think you've done anything wrong.'

Hannah says nothing. Nothing she can say will be what Olivia wants to hear.

'Do you remember what you told me not so long ago?' Olivia asks, leaning across the table. 'You said that when I'm older, when I've got kids of my own, I might finally understand you.' She pushes her chair back and stands, looking down at Hannah. 'You were wrong,' she says. 'I will never understand you. I never want to understand you.'

Hannah watches her daughter leave, but says nothing. Olivia hasn't changed; she is still her stubborn self, still the same girl who sees life through the eyes of a child. All Hannah has ever tried to do is keep her safe, and all Olivia has ever done is throw her efforts back at her, refusing time and time again to see the world for the awful place it is. She is on her own now, she thinks. Let her do what she will with her freedom.

TWENTY-EIGHT

OLIVIA

It is late August and they are basking in a heatwave that has generously stretched itself across the month, treating them to the kind of summer holiday that every child longs for. The park is packed and noisy, young families enjoying picnics on the grass and children screaming with delight at the jets that spray them with icy water at the splash pad that lies beyond the playground.

Olivia sits on a bench, Miss Johnson beside her. Rosie is in front of them, sitting cross-legged on the grass beneath a tree, an open book in her hands and her head bowed to the story.

'I never used to get it,' Olivia says, nodding in her sister's direction. 'Rosie and books. I used to think that while her head was stuck in those pages she was missing so much, but maybe that was the point. Is that why you like books, so you can escape?'

'Maybe. Sometimes.'

Olivia knows why Miss Johnson says nothing more. They have waited months for Olivia to speak about what has happened to her, but until now she has never felt ready. She has wanted to – she has always wanted to – but the words would never come out right. Sometimes she wasn't sure she would ever be able to find the right words.

Miss Johnson waits.

'What if she doesn't cope?'

'She'll be fine, I promise you. You girls are made of strong stuff.'

'Not Rosie. My mum.'

Miss Johnson looks at her sadly.

'I'm worried she won't cope in prison. What if they're awful to her in there?'

'Olivia,' Miss Johnson says, putting a hand on her arm. 'You mustn't do this to yourself. She won't be there forever, and they won't let anything happen to her.'

Olivia knows that no one else understands. Despite everything, Miss Johnson has never said a bad word about Hannah – not in front of Olivia, at least – but Olivia knows that she and Rosie are expected to hate her. It would be easier if she could, she thinks, but no matter how many times she has thought she might, the truth is that she doesn't, and she can't.

'Some terrible things happened to her,' she says quietly.

Miss Johnson pauses as though considering her response carefully. 'Some terrible things have happened to you, Olivia. And the sad thing is that sometimes bad things do just happen and there's nothing anyone can do to stop them. But it's how you react to the terrible thing that's important. It's what you do afterwards, that's what matters.'

Olivia says nothing. She understands what Miss Johnson is saying, and she knows that she is right.

'Miss Johnson?'

'Yes.'

'There's a wasp in your hair.'

Miss Johnson leaps from the bench as though she has already been stung, shaking her head in front of her so that her hair flies in all directions, flailing her hands. Eventually she stops, red-faced, and peers at Olivia from behind her hair.

'Is it gone?'

Olivia nods, trying but failing to suppress a giggle. When Miss Johnson sits back on the bench, she realises Olivia wasn't the only one watching her fit of panic, and the two of them laugh as she rearranges her hair.

'I really hate wasps. And you can call me Amy, remember. I'm off duty.'

Olivia smiles. Miss Johnson has told her this before, but calling her by her first name seems wrong, somehow disrespectful.

'Can I ask you something?'

Olivia nods.

'Why didn't you say anything sooner? You could have talked to someone at school.'

She is not the only person to ask the question, though she has taken longer to get to it than anyone else.

'I used to think about it, all the time,' Olivia tells her. 'Especially at night-time, when there was nothing else to distract me. I used to imagine just walking into class and telling someone, telling you, but I never could. It was like, if I said it out loud, then it was really real. I was really part of this crazy family, like something from a film. When I wrote it in that story you read, it was like writing about someone else's life. I still didn't have to admit that it was really me.'

She stops talking and watches as Miss Johnson's aunt, Lisa – their foster carer – crosses the park towards Rosie and leans down to pass her an ice cream. Rosie puts her book on the ground and takes it from her, and an exchange passes between the two of them.

'There's no place like home.'

'Sorry?'

'*The Wizard of Oz.* "There's no place like home." Rosie said it once, and I got what she meant. What if whatever else was out there was worse? I didn't want to go to a children's home. I didn't want Mum and Dad to go to prison. They're still my mum and dad. But then I realised how dangerous he was. That night …' She trails off, not wanting to have to think about what happened. 'I never meant to put Rosie in danger like that, making her run for help. I'd always planned to do it myself, but I couldn't. That night I really thought he could kill one of us, and I don't think I'd ever believed it until then.' She stops, swallowing a silent sob, and she feels Miss Johnson's hand return to her arm, her fingers just resting there. 'I didn't want to believe it.'

Miss Johnson looks at her sadly, and they are silent for a moment, lost in their thoughts as Lisa approaches them. She is carrying a second ice cream, which she hands to Olivia, its raspberry sauce running onto her fingers as it already starts to melt in the early afternoon heat.

'Right, miss,' Lisa says without sitting. 'You've made us wait long enough.' She licks the sauce from her fingers and gestures to Olivia's bag on the bench beside her. 'They're not going to open themselves.'

Olivia licks the melting ice cream and glances down at her bag and the envelope that is peeping from inside. She takes it out, still uncertain she wants to know what awaits her.

'Don't tell anyone at school I said this,' Miss Johnson says conspiratorially, 'but GCSE results aren't the be-all and end-all, okay? If you don't get what you're hoping for, you can resit.'

'The fact that you turned up and sat them at all is incredible,' Lisa adds.

Olivia nods silently. She still finds it difficult to accept compliments, never believing herself worthy of them. She just did what she needed to, as she has always done. She glances at Miss Johnson, who gives her a reassuring nod and smiles encouragingly as Olivia gives her the ice cream to hold. Then she reaches for the envelope and tears it open.

Dear Diary,

I'm sorry I haven't written in you for a while. I haven't
known what to say.

Something terrible has happened, something so bad
that I haven't been able to put

it into words. I feel dirty. It feels like time has just
stopped and my life is over. I

keep going back over that night, trying to work out
what happened, how I let it

happen, but I can't make any sense of it. I was just in
the wrong place at the wrong

time, I know that, but it feels as though I could have
stopped it. I should have been

able to stop it. I can't tell anyone about what happened.
My mother would kill me.

Michael knows – he has been amazing. If it wasn't for
him, I don't know what I

would have done. I wish I'd listened to him now and
not gone to that party. None of

this would have happened. I feel sick. I always feel sick.
I thought at first that it

was just the thought of what happened that was
making me feel this way, but now

I know different. I did the test this morning, I had to
steal one from the

supermarket when I was doing Mum's shopping. I
couldn't pay for it – she'd have

seen it on the receipt. I am so scared. I don't want this
thing inside me. It feels as
though I am carrying around an alien, a monster, and I
just want it to go away. I
could make it go away, but Michael tells me that I
shouldn't. He says that this is
something beautiful come from something terrible,
that we can make it work if I'll
let him. There aren't many men who would offer to do
what he is. I am so grateful
to have found him, and I never want to let him down
again. I'm going to keep it. I
will learn to feel differently, I suppose, in time. Michael
loves me, I know that. If I
hadn't already known, this would be more than proof
of how he feels. He can take
me away from this life, give me something so much
better. He can save me. I want
to be saved.

A LETTER FROM VICTORIA

Dear Reader,

I want to say a huge thank you for choosing to read *The Argument*. If you enjoyed it and would like to keep up to date with all my latest releases, just sign up at the following link. Your email address will never be shared, and you can unsubscribe at any time.

www.bookouture.com/victoria-jenkins

The idea behind *The Argument* was a simple one – a seemingly ordinary, everyday falling-out between a mother and daughter that turns out to be something far more sinister. The question over what goes on behind closed doors is a trope in psychological fiction, with family relationships and all their complications offering a broad scope of themes for writers to explore. With Olivia and Hannah, I hoped to create a relationship that to the outside world might appear normal and would be immediately recognisable to many mothers and daughters. Olivia is a stereotypically moody teenager, pushing her parents' boundaries and flouting the rules, while Hannah is an exhausted woman struggling to cope with her teenager's challenging behaviour.

In the news recently there was the story of an American couple who were guilty of keeping their thirteen children imprisoned in the family home, inflicting upon them a catalogue of physical and psychological abuse. Some of the couple's children had attended school, which raised questions about how no one – friends, teachers or other staff – noticed that something was amiss with these children's lives. It occurred to me that it is frighteningly easy for abuse, in all its forms, to be kept hidden beneath the 'right' appearance. When reading about the family and how their seventeen-year-old daughter managed to escape from the house and raise the alarm, what struck me was the fact that this girl – little more than a child, and kept younger than her years by her incarceration – loved her parents despite everything. She recognised their wrongdoings, their crimes, and yet she lived with the hope that things might change and that the mother and father she loved would one day come to love her in return.

The psychology of Hannah's character and what drives her behaviour was as interesting to explore as Olivia's. The manipulation and control she has experienced throughout her life – first by her mother, then at the hands of her husband – contribute to her belief that she is doing the right thing by her daughters and has their best interests at heart, but is it enough to excuse or justify the way she behaves? I'll let you decide.

I hope you enjoyed *The Argument*; if you did, I would be very grateful if you could write a review. I would love to hear what you think, and it really does make a difference helping new readers discover one of my books for the first time.

I love hearing from my readers – you can get in touch on my Facebook page, Twitter, Goodreads or my website.

Thanks,
Victoria Jenkins

victoriajenkinswriter

@vicwritescrime

victoriajenkins

ACKNOWLEDGEMENTS

A massive thank you to everyone at Bookouture, with special thanks to Jenny, my editor, who continues to be a huge support and source of confidence. Thanks also to my lovely agent, Anne, whose insight and experience are invaluable. Thank you to Noelle Holten, who promotes my books with untiring enthusiasm (and provides a constant source of entertainment via social media).

As always, the biggest of thank yous to my family – I wouldn't get many words written without you. In particular, thank you to my husband, Steve, who has to put up with my (sometimes fairly extensive) moments of panic and self-doubt. To Mia, who is the reason for everything I do, thank you for being the funniest, smartest, most beautiful little girl I could ever have hoped to have in my life. I am learning from you every day, and hoping I pass a little bit back too.

Although *The Argument* is a story about a mother and daughter, it is also a story about sisters – the infuriating and the inseparable. To my own infuriating younger sister, Kate – I don't know where I'd be without you. Thank you for always being there, for the in-jokes that no one else gets, and for always seeming to know when I need a reminder that I'm being an idiot. And for reading when you're 'not a reader', this one is for you.